The Casserole Widow

To order additional copies, please contact us.
BookSurge, LLC
www.booksurge.com
1-866-308-6235
orders@booksurge.com

KATHLEEN
S. MCCRACKEN

Lally

THE CASSEROLE
WIDOW

IN MY FATHER'S HOUSE

2004

The Casserole Widow

This Book Is Dedicated To My Family, My Friends, And Mama's Friends Who Have Encouraged Me By Sharing Their Stories With Me.

PROLOGUE
"Parting is Such Sorrow"
The Widow

It's been eighteen years since Mama died, sixteen years since Daddy married The Widow, and six years since we buried Daddy. The intervening events seem now more like a distant dream than reality. The Widow, The Casserole Widow, is moving away. A casserole widow is a lady who rushes to the side of a bereaved widower, bringing comfort in the form of a hot casserole with hopes of making a good match with the vulnerable, grieving, prosperous widower. When The Widow wrote a note published in the church bulletin, and the preacher called the congregation to bid her farewell at the alter, Bessie, my sister, and Jonelle, my brother's wife, were able to greet her without malice. I wasn't there. In our hearts we are truly able to wish her well. Time has eased the pain of losing our father before he died.

The blame and bitterness is gone. I will say, the note she wrote was a bit melodramatic, as I could have predicted, and brought back a little sting.

"Parting is such sorrow.

I have been a member of this church for a long time. I married and funeralized my beloved Buchanan here, so I have happy and sad memories. It has now become time that I start another phase of my life, so I am moving away. I shall never forget my good friends here and the many great services I have attended.

So... ... Au Revoir"

The Widow

I think I'll send her a card.

"In retrospect I wish we had wiped those attic shelves clean and taken everything in sight. We in our naiveté were trying to be fair"

Kathy Jean

CHAPTER 1

I remember putting my hands on my hips and surveying the attic. The faint odor of cedar mixed with the smell of burning dust as the tiny particles hit the hot, bare, bulb. It still looked junky, in spite of our long morning. The Christmas china was still stored in Bessie's old yellow pie safe. An old stack of mason jars from some long-forgotten canning project, probably fig preserves, stood piled haphazardly in a corner.

Mama and Daddy used to preserve figs from the huge fig tree by the corner of the carport. The tree, an offshoot from Grand Mama's, was planted on my birthday the fall after we moved into the "new" house, Mama's house. The figs were tiny and sweet. We would eat them directly off the tree, in preserves, or in homemade fig ice cream. Mama would peel and freeze them for Daddy. The frozen fruit was pink, luscious, with tiny seeds, coated with crystals of ice. I frankly thought that peeling them was a bit overkill, but enjoyed sneaking them occasionally from the freezer bags, so carefully tied with the little twists. I'm sure Mama knew I got into the figs, because I could not tie those twists as neatly as she could. Grand Mama's fig tree was by her two-story garage, an outbuilding. From the rickety old steps, we could pick figs all the way to the top of the tree.

Downstairs, in the front of the garage, was room for one car, and an assortment of tools, including a manual push mower. The floor was sandy. We used to play there, searching for doodlebug homes. We would take a small stick, stir around the little cone-shaped indention in the sand, and chant, "Doodlebug, doodle bug, your house is on fire", looking for the harmless bug that tickled your palm when you captured it. There was a coal bin, in the dark recesses of the garage. Buchanan used to "fetch" coal for the little fire Grand Mama always kept glowing in the winter.

Behind the parking area was storage where Grand Mama kept her chicken feed, fertilizer, and gardening supplies. She would let us feed the chickens. I was afraid of them, especially the roosters. I felt very brave slipping my hand into the hens' nests, sneaking the eggs out. I loved to feel the marble eggs Grand Mama kept in the nests; I guess to fool the hens into thinking there were still eggs there after we robbed the nests. I have an old alabaster egg still today. It feels cold and smooth and safe.

Daddy used to tell the story that once he and his cousins built an experimental aircraft that they were about to launch from the roof of that garage with his little brother, my uncle Elmore, as the test-pilot when Uncle Elmore was relieved of duty at the last moment by my frantic Grandmother. My mama used to say that Grand Mama must not have watched the boys very well. When I heard the stories of such wild escapades, I believe, remembering my own childhood and hearing now the stories of my grown children, that it may be a miracle that any child reaches adulthood.

Upstairs, above the garage area was a veritable treasure trove to us grandchildren. Grand Mama would allow us to go there and plunder at will. There were old high-heeled shoes, fancy hats, and dresses to tromp around in. There were various tools whose purposes were unknown to us, assorted pictures, antique and junk furniture, and of course Uncle Elmore's old skeleton, Gus. I think the bones were real human bones, or at least they told us that. Gus was a part of Uncle Elmore's medical school studies. Whenever I go into an antique store, the smell inevitably takes me back to that garage.

CHAPTER 2

"What should we do with the jars?" Bessie I wanted to take some of the bric-a-brac on the makeshift shelf along the wall, but didn't feel free to do so. I remembered when my Grandmother-in-law died suddenly and unexpectedly. Not only did Granddaddy lose his wife of many years, but he also lost a great portion of his material possessions. His three daughters swooped in the house like buzzards and stripped his house to the bare bones. We didn't want to do that. As I looked at each item, I wondered what it had meant to Mama. Mama saved everything and for everything she saved, she had a reason. What about those Chinese teacups? Did she save them because they are truly fine, or did they have some sentimental value that Mama never shared with us? When Bessie and I would have a yard sale, Mama would relent to part with a tiny fraction of her junk. We would offer to sell the broken nutcracker shaped like an old street vendor with his big, brightly painted red mouth open, ready to crack pecans. She'd say, "No, Kitty gave me that as a souvenir of her trip to the Bahamas and it might hurt her feelings if I give it away." She saved every gift, bridge prize, or souvenir that anyone ever gave her, I think. After she died we found some earrings that Buchanan had given her consisting of an old penny stuck with a blob of cement glue to the back of some grimy screw-on earring backs. I remember Mama wore them with pride and I remember how pleased Buchanan was. I can understand that part, but it is hard to believe that she kept them right on, unless of course, you knew Mama.

When I went to my kindergarten teacher's funeral, the minister alluded to her perchance for saving things and not letting her daughters "clean out." She made them take back into the attic sackfuls of things the girls had "helped" her sort. The minister said she felt that each item represented the love and friendship of her former students and friends. They were not junk. I know that is how Mama felt, too.

How could Daddy be so easily plucked by someone so different? The Widow is one of those types that would have engendered hostility in Mama too, and those types were few and far between. Mama was amiable and gracious, for the most part, but occasionally a woman like The Widow would arouse her distrust or even her ire. Mama particularly distrusted what she described as "too much sweetness and light." "Sweetness and light" refers to the kind of person that is overly goodie-goodie on the surface, but who is capable of unbelievable deceitfulness.

Mama was sentimental, and The Widow hasn't the faintest notion of how an attic could become so cluttered. She thinks it rather a sign of inefficiency. I heard that all she had in the attic of her condo when she moved to Daddy's house was a box of all-one-color Christmas ornaments. How boring!

Bessie and I both had a little pile of mementos we wanted to ask if we could keep. Bessie wanted some pieces of Mama's childhood tea set to go with what she already had. Mama had already given her the other pieces. I wanted to claim some flower vases.

At that time I had a rose bed with one dozen bushes. I had a dozen because one Valentine's Day my husband, Scott, the Scotchman, discovered the high price of cut roses and figured that it would be much cheaper over the long-haul to buy the bushes instead of cut flowers. Besides, the bushes had been on sale. They could have been a blue-light special. He loves specials. Never mind how much it would cost to buy all the various sprays, sprayers, and assorted manures and fertilizers roses require.

I worked hard with them for several years, but eventually was whipped by the Japanese beetles, and pulled all but the hardiest climbers. I suppose I kept them long enough to recoup the initial investment in the following Valentine's, Mother's Day, anniversary, and all other such flower giving occasions.

A few weeks before the clean up I had lots of roses blooming and thought that some spare vases would be great to have on hand. At that time, I didn't have the foresight to know that when my younger daughter Belle became a teenager, that rose vase shortage would no longer exist at our house. It seems teenage boys do not show the same reluctance to spend money on roses as does her daddy.

In retrospect, I wish we had wiped those attic shelves clean and taken everything in sight. We, in our naiveté, were trying to be fair.

By the time we finished plundering and sorting, the hall was cluttered with things from the attic we had chosen to ask if we could keep and some things that we figured Daddy and The Widow could not want. When we were in doubt, we left whatever it was in the attic for them to decide. Buchanan would come by to see if there was anything he might want. As a general rule Buchanan wanted no part of this! He, unlike Bessie and I, claimed not to be interested in household goods. However, he was obviously appreciative when we saved something for him. For example, there was an old wooden box we claimed. It turned out that Buchanan had spotted two of these at an antique store when he was shopping for a gift for JoNelle. He ended up giving one to Mama. He was proud to have that box back.

Jannie Mae would take off the rest—except for the craft materials in the old chifforobe in the middle bedroom. Jannie Mae did not like waste. She always knew someone who could use what Mama no longer needed. Later, when The Widow was about to discard Mama's old Winthrop yearbook and other pictures, thank heavens it was Jannie Mae's nature to check things out. She salvaged the pictures and took them to Bessie.

Sometime during the course of the morning, Daddy brought his bride-to-be by to "speak". *I suppose at this point I need to explain a little about Daddy. To understand Daddy would help shed light on the whole situation. You see Daddy, rather aptly named "Grand" by the first grandchild Anna Bet (a name he seemed to feel suited him, I might add) was a demigod of sorts in our county. He was, in his early days of practice, the only pediatrician in a three county area, and he made house calls. He was, at work, endlessly patient, understanding and kind. He was often paid in fresh collards, tomatoes, eggs and other farm products. He was an excellent diagnostician as well as smart, hard working, and good looking. Mama called him the "great white, Dr. Buchanan" when she was peeved with his attitude. When he walked the halls of Kingston Hospital, it was said that some of the nurses fluttered like silly schoolgirls. His word was law…at work and at home. He attracted children like a magnet attracts iron. Some say he attracted the Mama's, too. Mama said he had "bedroom eyes". His bright blue eyes could crinkle in laughter or grow steely with anger. Grand Mama had those same blue eyes but hers were gentle, yet alert.*

Mama arranged everything around Daddy. At home the telephone rang constantly: Christmas, Thanksgiving, all hours of the day and night. We were trained to answer the telephone properly, deflect calls when possible when he wasn't on call, but to never, never lie. I listened to untold symptoms. I know that the mama knew I was only a child, but I guess she needed to unload. I had to listen politely as some mother related bowel or throat problems.

"Dr. Buchanan's residence."

"I need to speak to Dr. Buchanan," the strained, worried voice would say.

"I'm sorry, but he isn't in right now. May I take a message and have him call you back?" There was always a pad, right by the phone, usually a promo from some drug company. Pencils were more elusive. Mama found this chain gadget like they have at the post office that hooked to the counter. It usually worked.

"Well, my baby has a fever and the croup. He keeps throwing up, and his skin is blotchy and he has diarrhea." The litany would go on and on.

Finally, I would say," I'm sorry but he isn't in. If you'll leave your number, I'll have him call as soon as he gets in." I'd carefully write down the number and he'd spend his first half –hour or so at home on the phone.

Some times he'd have to go back out and make a house call or meet someone at the hospital. Sometimes he'd let me ride. He would leave me in the car to read while he strode to the front door, black bag in hand.

His black bag was full of mysterious things- stethoscopes, odoscopes, tongue blades, even the dreaded syringes and needles. We were not allowed to touch it, but I always tried to sneak a look when he opened the bag. It smelled like band-aides when you first open them.

Due to experiences like this, I avoid any unnecessary contact today with the medical field. Many times we were frightened by what we heard. Looking back I know that Daddy truly believed that he was more important than Mama. After all, he was not only the breadwinner but also responsible for saving so many lives.

Unfortunately, we picked up that same attitude. When I get to heaven, first thing I want to do is apologize to Mama.

We were told repeatedly of his serious responsibilities as we were growing up. We felt that he was so important, more important than all the rest of us put together. We felt guilty if our needs came in conflict with his.

Also, we were told that after all his pressures at work, he needed to relax. He and Mama went "out" several times a week. Up until the time we were in college we had "baby sitters." Baby sitters told us the facts of life, town gossip, and one even demonstrated how to French kiss with her boyfriend. I know Mama and Daddy had no idea. We didn't tell. On weekends, Daddy hunted quail, fished, played golf, and generally absented himself. It was explained to us that Daddy needed this time to himself, because he was so wonderful. Didn't everybody say so? We believed that we would be incredibly selfish to ask for more of his time. We always craved Daddy's attention and tried to please him. Mama tried to make up for it, but she was spread thin. There was never any question about her priorities. He was first.

Once when I was a teenager, we were at a swim meet when Ed, who gave a great deal of his time to civic responsibilities and was our coach, asked me where Daddy was. Ed was one of Daddy's long time friends and his lawyer. I told him Daddy couldn't be there because he had to work. Ed commented, "He could be here if he wanted to". I remember feeling defensive but also feeling he was right.

I always admired Ed's multifaceted wife, Evelyn. She didn't cow-tow to Ed. She had the knack of getting people going and things accomplished. We were staying at Murrells Inlet one time and were all going out to a sandbar to go crabbing at low tide. Mama and Evelyn were paddling out in separate boats with all the children and paraphernalia including a playpen for Bessie and Evelyn's son, Walter. I was in the back of Mama's boat "helping" her paddle by dipping my paddle in the water and swirling it around and around.

We seemed to be going in circles. Evelyn's boat was making a beeline to the sandbar. I dared to compare our progress to Evelyn's. I asked, "How come Evelyn is so far ahead?"

Mama was not happy with me, and pointed out, "Kathy Jean, that paddle you are swirling in the water is NOT HELPING! Get it out of the water right now and maybe we'll get there too!"

Evelyn could be a beach bum or an elegant lady. She had impeccable, though expensive taste. Mama used to say she couldn't see how they spent so much money.

When Daddy got older he realized how much lawyers charge. It seems that for years, Daddy, the house call doctor, had treated all four of his children, free of charge and usually at their home. However, when Ed settled Grand Mama's estate, Daddy was shocked with the size of what he considered to be a whopping bill. I think Daddy expected the same special treatment he had given and that everybody thought about money the way he did. Daddy was truly hurt as he and Ed went way back. They both had ties to Marion and at the Citadel. They say Ed spent more time walking tours than in class when he was at the Citadel. One of his escapades had to do with crawling under the mess tables and "buttering" the officer's shoes. As the men told the tale, they would laugh uproariously. I guess you had to be there. I think Citadel men have lots of inside jokes.

Ed was lots of fun and didn't mind sharing free fatherly advice. Once when he was driving a station wagon full of us teenage girls on the swimming team to a meet, he took the time to explain to us why we should not use the word "crap". We had adopted it to use when we wanted to describe something unpleasant. We never thought of it as offensive. We had no idea it meant "something worthy of being in a toilet" as he defined it. We immediately took the word from our speaking vocabulary, at least in front of the adults!

Ed's willingness to work with youngsters had long-lasting positive effects. Scott feels that Boy Scouts, and Ed, his scout master, had a hand in rescuing him from unpleasantness at home and offering him hope for his future.

Being Daddy's child was not always easy. Pediatrician's children, like preacher's children are supposed to behave well. Because he was smart, we were supposed to be. Of course, there were those who thought we were "rich doctor's children".

Never mind that there were people who never ever thought to pay and mind you, he often took payment in vegetables. One summer, when I was in the seventh grade, too young to get a real job, but old enough to want to earn my own money, I worked at Daddy's office typing out old bills; the ones he only bothered to send once a year, because he knew they probably wouldn't be paid. I was shocked to see the folks on that list. Many of them had finer clothes and much fancier cars than we did. Daddy didn't turn patients away, though. He said children couldn't help how their parents were.

We admired him and craved his approval. We excused him for not attending dance recitals, music recitals, and baseball games. He couldn't possibly be at swim meets, honor society inductions or even at the ball field when Bessie was crowned homecoming queen.

Finally, Dr. Ambrose came to work with Daddy and had enough ego, good looks and medical skills to be able to work with Daddy. When Dr. Ambrose was drafted during the Vietnam War, Daddy held down the double practice for several years. That was hard on him and on the rest of our family. He was overtired and crabby most of the time.

Daddy was caring, super-responsible and intelligent. I think he kept a tight rein on his emotions. He didn't often express love and yet I always felt he loved me the best he knew how. He just wasn't able to show it, Grand Mama was like that, too. He once told me that his parents never told him they loved him. He didn't tell us either. I remember tears in his eyes, only two times: once, when he left me at college and again when he told us about the diagnosis of Buchanan's friend with leukemia.

When we ever met with Daddy's approval, we basked in it. He enjoyed helping us with math and science. He literally walked me through geometry. Sometimes he and some other daddies would have to consult one another to help us solve math problems. He was there for Buchanan and me more though, than he was for Bessie. I guess by the third child, he was less responsive. Bessie was like Mama. It seems like she had a real hard time getting Daddy to notice her.

Christmas seemed like a culmination of the "Grand" attitude. Daddy would always have a huge pile of presents from his patients. I used to feel sorry for Mama because she got so little in comparison, yet she appreciated her gifts – Daddy seemed to just take it for granted – and toss them aside. Until the day he died he was hard to please with a present. He bought what he wanted and was deluged by gifts on special occasions. So you see, Daddy basked in adulation. He needed his way, his worshippers, and his life to be the center of attention.

Looking back, what happened shouldn't seem so strange now.

He gave up his practice. He lost his vigor after lung cancer surgery that left him with breathing problems though it cured him. Finally, he lost his wife of forty years, who was always there to help make life run smoothly for him. He was facing reality. He was ripe for plucking by a Casserole Widow.

Daddy brought The Widow by to inspect our progress. She was dressed to the nines. Of course, Bessie and I were quite a contrast, all sweaty in our old ragged shirts and jeans. Believe me, we did not look like the heroines of those romance novels who slipped on their jeans and tee shirts, a little mascara, and looked great! In the heat and humidity, Bessie's curly hair was frizzing and my fine straight hair was lank and droopy.

After the widow finally left, Verda Lee, who was Daddy's

one time secretary, came by to pick up the craft materials to donate to the senior citizens center. She couldn't believe it when she learned that Daddy had actually brought The Widow to oversee us as we were cleaning out the attic and the upstairs closets. She felt that it was a personal intrusion on Mama's privacy.

She made us stop what we were doing, and demanded, "If something happens to me, and Sam is about to remarry, don't you dare allow another woman, under any circumstances to go through MY things. Promise me!

"We promise."

"Swear! Swear on your Mama's grave."

We swore. We were laughing, yet we were sad. I had felt the same way but thought that perhaps I was being a bit oversensitive. When Verda Lee expressed her thoughts aloud, I felt somewhat relieved and a little less selfish.

She made us promise, too, that if anything happened to her and Sam was about to remarry, we would help her daughter clean out. Cleaning out Mama's belongings was very personal. It made us remember, in a very real way, what she was like. Remembering only made the contrast between The Widow and Mama unavoidably clear and all the more painful.

CHAPTER 3
"There is a difference between hand-made and home-made." Mama

*A*lways the home economist, Mama loved a project. That's why she had so many leftover materials. She was always working on something---knitting, needlepoint, or smocking. She enjoyed the sociability of them. She was rather a perfectionist, and seemed to seek more help on her project than she probably actually needed. I think some of this was an attempt to relieve loneliness. She enjoyed working with people in the craft shops, taking lessons, planning, shopping for appropriate materials, and sharing with others what she had learned to do. Mama considered herself an able teacher, and she was.

Sometimes though, she would even try to teach things she couldn't do herself, like ski on slalom. She felt like she could analyze things and see what we were doing wrong. I have to say she caught a lot of grief about this.

Rose, one of my childhood friends, later known as one of the "The Kingston Girls", was one of Mama's smocking cohorts. Rose really got into it when she adopted Elizabeth. Rose was a lady like Mama who had a gift of making those around her feel great. She helped teach Mama how to smock. My nieces, who went through the toddler stage while Mama was in her smocking phase, were grandly dressed little young ladies, thanks to Mama and Rose. I remember the last Easter dress she smocked for Belle; as usual, she wanted it to be perfect. Mama used to say that there was a difference between hand-

made and homemade. She just wouldn't give it to Belle until she felt it was up to her standards, and she was having difficulty in getting the hem just so. I finally bought a store-bought dress for Belle to wear for Easter. Mama gave her the dress, perfectly hemmed, later that summer. Her painstaking efforts were clearly reflected in its quality. It was beautiful. I still have it. See? We keep things.

Before Scott and I moved to Greenwood, we called Rose and Ashley to get the scoop on the town. They encouraged us to come and we appreciated it. Moving into a small southern town can be hard if you don't know anybody. We moved to her husband's hometown of Greenwood right after Mama died. When I called Rose before we moved to check out Greenwood, I knew she would be honest with me. She had married into an old Greenwood family and lived in her husband's family home place; a rambling, somewhat decrepit, old brick home from I would guess the early twenties. It was, as we say in the low country, arrogantly shabby. It wreaked of old money. Rose incorporated the old family antiques and created a welcoming, warm home. Rose and I would hit the road together for our biannual Kingston Girls' reunions. Half the fun would be getting there. One time I remember, when Belle was about six, we were traveling together to the beach when the inevitable "I need to go to the bathroom," echoed from the back of the van. We said "Sure," and proceeded to talk past the exits with rest rooms, as well as the rest stop. Belle finally wailed in desperation, "I have GOT to go!" We would get so busy talking that often we would completely miss exits, as well. It's a wonder we ever got where we were going. Rose had a great sense of fun that was infectious. Her beautiful porcelain skin and silky, curly, blond hair that stayed beautiful, even when her hair grew back after her bouts with chemo. Now, whether it was always naturally blond, I doubt, because she was definitely the type to experiment for the fun of it, but whatever the case it was beautiful. The sense of mischief in her eyes belied her angelic look. She had a collection of jokes for any occasion. Any story she told had a sense of hilarity to it. She could find humor in the most mundane. She had a zest for life that kept her always involved in something interesting, productive, or fun. Above all, she was gracious, kind, and caring, with enough of a bite to her tongue to make her human. Rose also had a sense of appreciation for the ordinary. She loved sweet rose-scented hand lotion, crisp white embroidered sheets, and vines with flowers on them.

She was a lot like Mama. As her illness progressed, we decided to have a spring "Kingston Girls" get-together in Greenwood. Rose had just had some surgery and was not able to travel, so everyone came to her. We laughed, and hooted and carried on, telling the same old stories as usual.

We especially enjoyed seeing for real, the parked tractor-trailer that belonged to her mother-in-law. Their home, which was by the way, located right next door to Rose, had been damaged in a fire. While the home was undergoing repairs, the Judge and his wife hit upon the idea of storing their belongings in the back of a tractor-trailer. It was a great solution. It was spacious, easy to move. The only problem was that they never emptied it. It became a permanent fixture. Apparently, china, pictures, furniture and all sorts of valuables are still stored there. Even Mama was not quite that bad about saving stuff. After we all left, Rose said that her husband rather quizzically asked, "Is this all you ladies do?" He just could not understand. I don't think any of the men do.

When we moved to Greenwood, Rose introduced us to her friends, invited me to visit her infamous bridge club and paved the way for us to make the transition as smooth as possible when you move to a small southern town. She is the one who pointed out to me the difference in upstate people and lower state people. In the upstate you are considered a son-of-a-bitch until you prove otherwise and in the lower part of the state you are accepted until you prove you are a son-of-a-bitch. Mama was definitely the lower-state type.

During the last months of Rose's illness, she and I had planned a trip downstate. She wanted to visit her mother. The remnants of a hurricane were blowing through the state. Do you think that stopped Rose? Of course not, she insisted that we travel as planned. Off we went into the storm. I prayed a lot, and figured we would make it, or have fun trying. I would have never made the decision to travel in that weather, but that was Rose. She was not afraid. She was able to help teach me that lesson that my mother could not.

Mama had a real fear of traveling, particularly alone. Unfortunately, she passed that fear on to me. She had a traumatic experience that made her fear understandable. Mine was more unreasonable. I knew that, but could not change. Later, it was fortunate that the change had come, for when Daddy was very ill, in his last months I needed to travel alone, and was able to do so, thanks to Rose and some very fervent prayers.

The Kingston Girls all gathered in Greenwood for Rose's funeral, all proudly wearing our single daisy, the symbol of the Girl Scouts. Our friendships began as we all were in Girl Scouts together. We began as Brownies in second grade. Edie, our smartest hometown friend turned florist, provided the flowers.

Mama's terrible experience involving traveling happened when she was a freshman at Winthrop College. Mama had grown up in the depression. She was fortunate enough to have had the where-with-all to even attend college. She was an only child and had left her beloved Charleston to attend the all girls' college. Her last name was obviously German, and during the early forties, was not exactly your passport to acceptance. In fact, one of the professors who was helping her with her registration said that Rahtert could not be her last name because he had never heard of such a name. She was anticipating with great happiness her first visit home for the Thanksgiving holidays. Her mother was driving, alone, to pick her up. The drive was a long one for that day; over 200 miles on what I'm sure were back roads.

Certainly there were no four-lane interstates then. My grandmother had pernicious anemia, which in those days was a very serious illness. Perhaps she was very tired. Whatever the circumstances, she was hit and killed by a big truck on her way to get my mother.

My Granddaddy said he always felt responsible for her death because he felt he had to work instead of going with her. What was ironic was that when Granddaddy, years later, in his early fifties, had a serious heart attack; the company did not feel the same loyalty toward him. He was let go immediately.

My mother would never talk about the accident, but I can only imagine how horrible it must have been for her, all packed and ready to go home, waiting and waiting, only to be told by one of her classmates of the terrible tragedy. I think Mrs. Hucks from Aynor, was the one who had to tell her. Subsequently, Buchanan, Bessie and I became friends with her children. Think of having to be alone and far away from home and having to cope with such news? I can certainly understand her terror of being alone in a car, or of us being alone. The fear was so very tangible that she passed it right on to me. It has taken years for me to get over it, even knowing how irrational it is.

Granddaddy and Mama's mother had a fascinating love story. I wish I knew more of the details. I have made up many stories in my mind about their courtship. They were always passionate and exciting. My Grandfather was the grandson of a German immigrant in Charleston, who had been a daring blockade-runner in the War Between The States. Granddaddy was proud of his heritage and the Holy City. He loved to take us on tours and give us history lessons. He told stories about the brave feats of his Grandfather as he outmaneuvered the Yankee sailors off the coasts of North and South Carolina.

Her well-to-do-family sent my grandmother, Anne, from West Virginia to Ashley Hall, a finishing school on the peninsula. She was an accomplished musician, who played the piano for silent movies. She *was quite a beauty as well. They may have sent her to Ashley Hall to separate her from an unsuitable beau. Apparently they were rather hard to please. She and granddaddy fell in love, but his family was not deemed a suitable match for her, either. They eloped. She was promptly disowned. Later, she was reconciled with her family, but things were never the same.*

When I was sixteen, Granddaddy gave me two rings that belonged to her, a diamond and a ruby. He told me he gave them to me because I was her namesake and he wanted me to remember her. When Anna Bet, my daughter, was sixteen I gave her the ruby, since a ruby is the birthstone for July. I gave the diamond to Belle, my youngest daughter, when she was sixteen. We like to keep jewelry in the family.

Remembering her, I have wondered from time to time if flirting is inherited or learned. Mama told me that her mother told her that the man in a relationship should always believe that he loves the woman more than she loves him. Unfortunately, neither Mama nor I were able to pull that one off. Whatever the case, both Mama and Belle developed flirting to a high art. Mama used to encourage me to flirt with the bag boys at the grocery store for practice. She would say that this was a safe and useful place to practice. I guess I was more like my more reserved Grand Mama Bethea. I never was much of a flirt.

My Grandmother Anne's mother had a child, Marjorie, about the same time that Mama was born. Since my Mama's mother died before her parents, and Mama was so far away from her grandparents who were from Charleston, West Virginia, when they died they left their considerable estate to Marjorie. My granddaddy always felt like this was all his fault. When I think about it, my unfortunate Granddaddy carried around a lot of guilt, didn't he? Granddaddy married in less than a year after my Grandmother's death. When he died he was buried beside his first wife, Mama's mother. When Kaye died, she was buried on his other side.

Kaye's funeral was another story. By then The Widow and Daddy were married. Of course, they chose not to go to the funeral. It always amazed me that when The Widow wanted or needed to do something, there was always a way, but when it was an important event in our family or among Daddy's old friends, they never seemed to manage. The only exception I can think of was Anna Bet's wedding. Daddy especially liked Anna Bet I think, and they made the trip to her wedding. Anna Bet was pleased that he came and gave her away. She still talks of this with great affection and fondness. It really was a shame that the younger grandchildren did not get to see the more caring side of Daddy. I remember Leslie saying after Grand's funeral, "Were they talking about Grand?" For a man who spent most of his life caring for and healing sick children, what an irony!

CHAPTER 4
"In my Father's house are many mansions."
John 14:2

Kaye, my granddaddy's second wife, died on Christmas day. We went to Charleston for the funeral the next day. She had been very sick and her death was not unexpected. I think she just hung on to get through Christmas. Through the years after Granddaddy died, we came to understand the stepchildren's feelings. Kaye was good to us, but her heart was with her own children and great-grandchildren. I suppose in our own busy ways we had just drifted further and further away. She had been very sick.

The funeral was not an unduly sad event for us. By then, it was more of a duty sort of thing. The services were held in the old funeral home in the city, the same as Granddaddy's. We met Buchanan and JoNelle, Bessie and Lou, and all the cousins there. We settled ourselves near the back of the elegant, musty old funeral parlor. The maroon carpet was, appropriately for Charleston, slightly worn. Thick, velvet pew pillows and heavy draperies added to the somber and slightly musty atmosphere of the room. Strains of organ music filled the room. The faint odor of flowers mingled with the dusty smell. The old brass fixtures with beveled glass and domed bulbs hung low from the ceiling.

Suddenly above the quiet mourners from a balcony, not unlike a box at a theater, burst forth an off-key duet, a rendition of the old funeral favorite "How Great Thou Art." The tremulous voices whined over the mourners. You know how sometimes when you know it is a most *inappropriate time to laugh, you laugh? Well, the cousins exchanged glances and started to snicker. The aunts tried to look stormily at them but it was very hard, since it was all we could do ourselves to keep from giggling aloud. Soon the group was silently laughing, shoulders shaking, almost uncontrollably. Bessie tried to cover up with a cough and ended up going into a choking spasm.*

We finally calmed down as the service began. Unfortunately for us the minister predictably intoned, "In My Father's house are many mansions". I whispered to Bessie that I hoped mama was not right next door to Kaye. We lost it again.

On the way to the gravesite, we laughed like a bunch of preteens. When we got to the cemetery, it was worse. It had recently rained and Charleston is not much, if any, above sea level. The ground was extremely soggy. As we walked to the gravesite, our high heels sank into the ground, pulling up with a little sucking sound. In Charleston it is the custom for the family not to leave until the grave is covered. They couldn't cover Kaye's until they pumped out the water. To the rhythmic sound of the sump-pump, we tried to be respectfully mournful.

It was hard to keep our composure as we watched the frail, whimpering Will, Kaye's grandson, being comforted by his life-partner Brett. Brett was so strong, yet tender. This was our first experience with an openly gay couple. We tried to be cosmopolitan and open-minded but we couldn't help but gape. Thankfully, the grave was at last covered and we could leave.

We left the funeral and went to The Market in Charleston where I acquired my first sweet-grass basket. We used to pass stand after stand in front of the houses with blue trim as we traveled to Charleston. The blue trim was to keep away the Plait-Eye, a most evil of evil spirits. Daddy would never, never stop. He was always in a hurry to either get there or to get home. Bessie got her first basket when she was in fifth grade. She asked for it for her birthday. One Christmas, years later my friend Sarah had a friend of hers from McClellanville make smaller ones for all the nieces, and big ones for all the Aunts. I'm afraid they will soon become a lost art, not to mention that sweet-grass is becoming more and more scarce. Sweet-Grass Charleston baskets remind me of trips to see Granddaddy and Kaye.

Kaye left all of her and Granddaddy's estate to her daughter, too. Granddaddy had been adamant that Mama's inheritance was not to go to the other side. He had told us so. Is there a pattern here?

In a way, Mother's attitude toward Kaye was what sort of set the tone for us to assume a polite attitude toward The Widow. Like Daddy, Granddaddy married shortly after his first wife's death. Mama did not view Kaye as her Mother. I know she felt displaced by her, especially when they sold her mother's home on the peninsula and moved across the Ashley. Mama never felt at home with them. Kaye had a young daughter, and I know Mama felt like she didn't belong in their little family group.

She often reminded us when we didn't seem to appreciate her or our home. Like when we didn't do our chores to suit her. She knew what it was like not to have a home. "You should appreciate our home. I hope you are never in a situation where you don't have one." We would call this her "rant and rave" mood and just roll our eyes, not understanding at all where she was coming from. I had to be much older to begin to know what she meant. I'm sorry to say The Widow taught me this lesson as well. I must say that our experience was not as tragic, though. Buchanan, Bessie, and I all had our own homes and families by now.

I think the tragedy in Mama's early life helped her become the caring compassionate person she was. She was able to visit the bereaved, laugh with the lonely, and comfort the sick.

When Elsie, Betty's mom, was so sick with her cancer treatment, Mama would go, carrying armloads of materials and threads, to sit with Elsie. They would work on a project to while away the time when Elsie was too weak to get out much. Elsie had lost her first *husband to an untimely heart attack when he was in his early forties. She remarried, a somewhat shady fellow, from Little River. Later, when his character became apparent to Elsie, she chose to stay in her own home in Conway most of the time. Some years later, her second husband just disappeared! I don't remember the details exactly, but I think someone was convicted of his murder, before they even found his body. I'm not sure where they finally found his body, or even if they did. Betty, who by the way was one of the Kingston girls, lost her husband to an untimely heart attack also. Maggie, another of the Kingston girls, and Hayward her husband, more or less took on the responsibility of helping Betty and her children. Hayward and Betty's husband were Citadel buddies.*

CHAPTER 5
"The cobbler's daughter has no shoes."

*M*aggie and Hayward seem to be a good match. Both came from well-respected, prosperous families. No one could accuse either of them of gold digging. Maggie's mama was a Bailey and her father was the local ophthalmologist. In fact, Maggie typed old bills for her Daddy the same year that I typed Daddy's. I guess our Daddies talked this over and decided this would be a good way to keep us busy and to teach us lessons in economics. The main lesson was that just because people owe you money doesn't mean they'll pay. I never understood how Dr. Marsh could even have had overdue bills. If he thought a person couldn't pay he didn't charge them. He exempted all preachers, teachers, medical professionals and who knows else from fees. He excluded more than he charged, it seemed to me.

One time Maggie, a whole bunch of friends and I were in Daddy's office for our mandatory P.E. physicals. The last thing on the checklist was vision. Daddy lined us all up at the end of the long hall where he did the vision screening. He told us to read the bottom line. One by one, they did, until he came to me. He said, "Read the bottom line". He had his pen ready to check off vision. "I can't," I said,

He said, "I SAID read the bottom line"

"I can't"

"Read the next one then"

"I can't see that one either".

Thoroughly frustrated he said, "Kathy Jean, quit showing off for your friends".

Tearfully, I said
"I really can't see it, Daddy"
"Dammit," he said, "Read the top line!"
"I can't see it, Daddy."
"You are going straight to Dr. Marsh's office if you don't go ahead and read that eye chart".

By then I was embarrassed and crying. When Dr. Marsh talked to Daddy later he said, "My God, the child is blind. I don't see how she has done so well in school." I guess I did well because I talked a lot and the teachers always put me in the front of the room.

Daddy was so ashamed of himself, he let me get two pairs of glasses – a red rhinestone studded pair and a mother-of-pearl cat-eye looking pair. Today they would really look tacky, but then I thought they were glamorous.

My friend Jane tried to fake poor vision to get some glasses, too, because she loved my glamorous ones! Dr. Marsh quickly caught on to that. She ended up with a pair of glasses with clear lenses. Dr. Marsh made them for her, free of charge, because he had a big heart and had never seen someone who wanted glasses so bad!

Maggie and the medical auxiliary had an interesting experience at Daddy's house, or "her" house as it later became. Daddy was not much into active participation in clubs and such, but The Widow loved the status she thought being in the medical auxiliary provided her. It seems they were having a luncheon of some sort and she offered to have it at her house. She wouldn't let them move the chairs from around the serving table. It was very awkward to reach over the chairs to serve the plates. At the end of the luncheon, she insisted that each person take their own serving dishes home to wash. They said that when The Widow left the kitchen and went to another part of the house that the women sneaked and washed their dishes.

That following summer after the eye examination I got prescription sunglasses for water skiing. I have several pairs of glasses at the bottom of the Waccamaw River for future archeologists to recover.

THE CASSEROLE WIDOW

My gym teacher thought catching the pediatrician's daughter's half-blindness on a required school screening was hilarious. I guess it was a case of the cobbler's daughter having no shoes. Whatever the case, it was a miracle to me to see clearly. The downside was that everyone was no longer beautiful. Myopic vision renders everyone beautiful.

CHAPTER 6
24 divided by 3 = 8

We emptied the Christmas closet. When the grandchildren came along, we used the closet in Bessie's old bedroom as the Christmas closet. It was kept locked at all times. Whenever Santa Claus found something, he put it in the Christmas closet, away from snoopers. Bessie and I were both notorious snoopers ourselves as children. We knew to hide things out of our own homes if we wanted to insure Christmas surprises for any of our offspring who may have inherited our penchance for snooping. We soon had repercussions from this. Early in the fall shortly after the closet was "closed", Bessie had found some fancy, decorated sweatshirts on a trip to Atlanta that she knew Lori and Leslie would love. Not having the closet available any more, she put the shirts in her bedroom in an old trunk. She had to temporarily move the trunk out of the bedroom when she moved the Victorian sofa into her bedroom. Of course Lori and Leslie opened the trunk and discovered their Christmas surprises. We may have inherited this from Daddy. Grand Mama said that he always cut into her pies and cakes if he could find them and that he would turn the kitchen upside down looking for them. She said that her best hiding places were out in the open. Once, she simply put the cake in the center of the kitchen table in a cake dish and he could not find it.

The Victorian sofa is also a part of the stolen furniture story. The Widow wanted to remove Mama's stuff in the living room and replace it with hers, which she thought was better. The Widow had claimed not to like antiques. She wanted to clear out Mama's living room and replace the antique furniture, most of which belonged to Grand Mama.

Of course, we found that her original dislike of antiques did not extend to the antique sterling silver flatware that used to belong to Aunt Daisy. Somewhere along the line, after Daddy and The Widow had been married several years, we decided that we would make a play for Mama's silver flatware. Like her china, she had invested a lot of time and money completing her set of silver flatware. She decided to convert all her silver to Aunt Daisy's Old Colonial pattern. She would go to the antique shows and swap her Chippendale or Old Violet. For some reason she wanted a 24 place setting of the Old Colonial. (24 divided by 3 = 8?) She had collected her set with some pieces of the other silver to spare. She always encouraged us to "complete our silver". She would often pick up pieces for Bessie, JoNelle and me in our various patterns. I was appointed by the group to approach Daddy about leaving the silver to us, since he was apparently about to turn everything else in the house over to her. When The Widow found out what we had done, she put the silver in zip lock bags and stormed over to JoNelle's and left them on her back steps. She didn't leave it all, though. I wonder what happened to the rest of it. JoNelle has what is left.

CHAPTER 7
"Stick to the Classics." Mama

We used to tease Mama about the Victorian sofas. She used to always say that they certainly were not what she would have chosen, but that she should be frugal and make use of what she has been given. When we were dividing the things in the living room, we all claimed not to want the Victorian stuff, particularly the two sofas. When we drew straws, Bessie lost and got the maroon velvet one, JoNelle came in second and won the blue moiré sofa, and I won the two velvet chairs in which no one could possibly sit comfortably. I used one of them for a while in my entrance hall to hold pocketbooks or coats for visitors, or to put stuff I needed to remember to take to the car. When we moved back to Kingston I gave them to Anna Bet. I suppose there is some poetic justice in that today Victorian furniture has come into its own again. I still don't like it though.

Mama taught us to use what we have and to work around it. I suppose that is why Bessie, JoNelle and I have to go for the "Shabby Chic" look in our own décor. We go eclectic. That's how we can mix a primitive chest that came from the old farm and was built by hand using cedar trees that were cut down when the land was cleared, in the same room with an ornate Victorian table and a traditional lamp. This way you stick with what you have and still try to maintain some semblance of order. "Stick to the classics" was Mama's byword when we were thinking of buying something new.

I have been keeping house for over thirty years now and I guess I learned that lesson well. I can count on my fingers the furniture I have bought, and most of it has been "classic".

A month or so after we cleaned out the closets and attic, Daddy asked us to go ahead and take the living room and dining room things that we were going to get, and we did. It was our understanding that she was going to use her things in the living and dining rooms. The Widow had decided that she would keep the den just as it was, even though she let us all know she hated blue. Already the martyr!

Bessie, JoNelle, and I sat down and wrote out what each of us would like to have. Again, I think Buchanan was trying rather wisely, to stay away from the whole affair. We had each just furnished our own dining rooms. We told Daddy that we would like to store the buffet and table and chairs for our children later because none of us had room for them. When Mama gave us furniture, it was always "on loan". It was ours forever if we wanted it, but if not; we were to give it back to her. Bessie, JoNelle and I still trade around furniture.

The widow decided to go ahead and use the table and chairs, and later had the buffet redone and put in the front hall. It looked so much better there than her early Heilig Meyers with the yellow cushioned velour seats like you see in the furniture store ads on Labor Day.

I must add that The Widow's distaste for antiques was not long-term. Later, Mama's simple yet elegant mahogany dining room table and chairs disappeared and were replaced with more fancy ornate ones. The same thing happened to the lovely desk Mama had in the den. She had saved her Christmas money Grand Mama had given her and shopped all the antique stores until she found the perfect piece. One day after I moved back to Kingston, I was browsing in an antique store downtown with my friend Harriette, Kitty's daughter, who was looking for more things to furnish her family's old home place on the river. I struck up a conversation with the proprietor, Archie. He revealed that from time to time he would go to Daddy's, haul off a piece, and sell it on consignment for The Widow. I don't know what Daddy thought about that. I know how I felt that day. Mad as a hornet!

After we moved the stuff out, Daddy went up to the drug store and told everyone there that he and The Widow had to go to Hemingway and buy all new furniture for the living room and dining room because his children had stolen all of his. I think he was trying to be humorous, but some of those listening took it literally. He did, indeed, buy some new furniture, but not because he had to. The Widow did nothing to correct this mistaken image.

At work a few days later, one of my brother-in-law Lou's secretaries asked him if it were true that the children had really come in the house and taken all Daddy's furniture. Lou, who is usually very even-tempered, was livid. He was ready to haul it all back to Daddy's and sit it under the carport. Since I lived out of town, it was easy for me to dismiss all of this, and Buchanan doesn't really set much store in what gossips might say.

With Bessie it was a different story. She said that she was embarrassed when she was out in public because she felt like people were looking at her and thinking that she was a neglectful daughter and a thief. I could see how she felt. We were feeling the losses more and more. We had lost our mother, and now were losing our reputations, our security and our way of life. We didn't know it then but we eventually lost Daddy for a while too.

CHAPTER 8
"What goes around comes around." Mama

The emptiness of the closets reflected this feeling. The old cedar chest in Buchanan's room was empty, too. *I recalled a time when Bessie, JoNelle, and I were helping Mama clean up Buchanan's room. Daddy used to say that Buchanan could shoot the President on national TV and Mama wouldn't believe it. Well, we were cleaning out the closet, and in an old trunk he had when he went to Viet Nam, we found a plastic bag with what looked like old potpourri, but I'm pretty sure it wasn't. Mama just said, "Oh, the army issued it to all the boys." Yeah, right!*

The closet had been full of old "classic" clothing. The ones Mama saved were the ones whose fabrics were especially beautiful or serviceable or whose style was sure to come back, some day, according to Mama. There were woolens, leathers linens, silks—no polyesters or blends. There was the dress she wore to Bessie's wedding, weeks after her by-pass surgery. It would be hard to forget that dress and how proud we were when she was able to walk down the aisle on Buchanan's arm.

We had been so upset. That was the last time we cleaned together, like this. Before she left for Charleston from the back of the ambulance, she asked us in a weak voice, "Please straighten the house." We took her literally and must have hauled off a truckload of junk then. It was all we knew to do. The doctors warned us that she might not even make it to Charleston in the ambulance. The wedding was coming up. I was expecting. The week of her surgery we sat around the dining room table writing invitations with some of Mama's friends. We just went on the faith that everything was going to be fine, and it was. We were taught to "carry on" and carry on we do. When Mama came home from the hospital, Anna Bet, who was about three at the time, took her by the hand and lovingly led her to her bed and told her it was "nap time" She loved Mama so!

Now, like Mama's final illness, we felt that what was happening was final, irrevocable. We were powerless to stop the progression. We were being carried in a direction we did not want to go. The only way we could see to slow the momentum would be to act in ways that would go entirely against the way we were brought up, not only by Mama, but also by Grand Mama, too. Even then, we still would probably not stop the wedding. We thought we would end up feeling even more rejected and frustrated. At the time, we felt that by choosing the route we did, we could try to maintain our dignity and upbringing. We would remain the gracious, Southern ladies we were trained to be.

At first when folks asked how I felt about Daddy remarrying, I would say that I was pleased, and I was. I thought, "Won't it be great for Belle to have a grandmother?" I knew that although Anna Bet and BJ would remember Mama, Belle might not. All children need loving grandparents. Scott's mother died almost exactly a year before Mama. The last time I saw Mama dressed up was at his mother's funeral. In fact she was noticing at that time the symptoms of what we were to soon learn was a terminal disease. I felt that my children could really appreciate a "new" grandmother. I did not want Daddy to be lonely. I felt relieved that Bessie, Buchanan and I would have help with Daddy. Bessie especially, could turn more attention to her own children.

CHAPTER 9
"Don't forget who you are." Grand Mama

I remember Mama saying that although she was not always fond of Kaye's ways, she was glad Granddaddy had someone to be with him, and for that reason she could live with any personal feelings of dislike she had toward Kaye for the sake of Granddaddy. Kaye was not unkind. She just wasn't Mama's mother. The least we could do was to follow her lead, I thought.

Besides, she perked Daddy up. He started getting out, traveling a bit. We had been worried that he would just lie up in his bed, do crossword puzzles and deteriorate, which he eventually did anyway. Some years before Mama's last illness, Daddy had surgery for lung cancer. Although the cancer was caught in time, he still did not have the stamina and energy he wanted, and he seemed too depressed to build himself back up. The idea of marriage seemed great! What changed?

Gradually I began to perceive that The Widow did not see us included in her role as Daddy's wife, being a grandmother to his grandchildren or being in any way motherly toward us.

Bessie saw it first, I think. She heard bits and pieces of gossip around town. Bessie's mother-in-law knew The Widow's family in Green Sea, where they both grew up on farms. The Widow ran off with her own Sister's fiancé! Later she claimed not to know who Clarimon was, an absolute absurdity. Very few people who grow up in a community the size of Green

Sea "forget" their upbringing and their neighbors unless I suppose they want to forget, or want to hope that others don't remember.

I understand The Widow grew up on a tenant farm. They say you could see the chickens under the house through the cracks in the floor. They say she was saddled with many farming and child-rearing responsibilities and was anxious to better herself.

The weekend before she announced her engagement to Daddy she spent the weekend in Washington, D.C. with another eligible bachelor. I guess she didn't think this widower was quite as prosperous or else as gullible as Daddy. This came from Me Maw, Buchanan's mother-in-law. Me Maw is in The Widow's Sunday school class. They keep tabs on everything that goes on, in and out of the church.

Me Maw's relationship with our Daddy went all the way back to Daddy's medical school days. She is originally from Kingston but was in training in Charleston when Daddy's cousin, Montgomery, who had settled there from Marion, was encouraging Daddy to settle in Kingston also.

Mama and Montgomery's wife were very different personalities. Claudia had a sardonic, droll personality. She was a Phi Beta Kappa at Duke and everybody knew it. Montgomery deferred to her. I can still picture her squinting her eyes, asking pointed questions as she looked up from a book she was reading. During the last weeks of Mama's illness, Claudia came by to visit. Mama remarked, "I'm really starting to worry about myself. Even Claudia is being solicitous."

Let's get back to Me Maw. Me Maw agreed at that time to help Daddy set up his practice here. She was his first office nurse. His office was in downtown Kingston. I remember the steep stairs going upstairs. Mama said that when they first moved to Kingston they were so broke that they had to charge their groceries at the grocery store around the corner from his office.

She told about how one Christmas Grand Mama gave her and Aunt Clara each a fur coat. First of all, the idea of a fur coat from Grand Mama Bethea seemed way out of character. Secondly, Mama said she felt odd charging groceries and wearing a fur coat. She didn't like to wear coats much. She thought, in our climate, coats were too much bother. I agree.

The Widow may have been what we call a "casserole widow". Casserole widows watch the obituaries and listen to the local gossip to see who has died and left a lonely, well-to-do-widower. Then they take a casserole to the house, as soon as possible, to initiate a possible relationship. It seems that is what The Widow did. She may have been one of those at the hospital who made eyes at Daddy. I don't know. Scott's mother, who was a R.N., said she was really hard to get along with when she was in charge of housekeeping there. I've always wondered how one so prissy could be in charge of housekeeping.

Apparently, Kingston is still full of casserole widows. A friend of mine, whose wife recently died said he had so many casseroles that he was running out of freezer space and he has a huge freezer.

She also ingratiated herself with the drugstore crowd. The drug store is right by the old hospital and by what used to be Daddy's office. When the hospital moved out on the highway between Kingston and Myrtle Beach, the drugstore stayed put. When I was a teenager, we all hung around the drugstore after school and on weekends. They had a grill and soda foundation with stools that spin around at the counter and several booths, straight out of the 50's. Daddy used to get irritated with me and the other teen-agers for riding around and hanging out at the drugstore. He called us drugstore cowboys. He said that we interfered with legitimate customers. He said it was a waste of good time. Later, where did he go every morning at 9:00 a.m. sharp? The drug store. Nothing, I tell you nothing interfered with his trips to the drugstore, short of hospitalization or death. Was Daddy right about the drugstore being a waste of good time? Probably not, but the rules that apply to him don't always apply to others. That is where The Widow continued to pursue Daddy. As I said before, she got herself into this crowd, maybe for just such a purpose.

At the drugstore, he would sit around with a bunch of his old cronies and drink coffee. There was the retired cynical doctor who always dressed in suits, which seemed to match his stiff personality. There was Ella, the husband collector who had buried three husbands, the alcoholic druggist who loved Ginkgo trees and various others who wandered in and out on a more or less regular basis. It was a motley crew, but they all seemed to enjoy meeting one another, looking after one another and catching up on the gossip. I remember how Grand Mama used to enjoy her trips to the drugstore and to the post office in Marion. Today, I see retired folks hanging around the lunch counter at Wal-Mart and think to myself, I bet they wish they had an old timey drugstore counter to hang around. Daddy would come home with all sorts of gossip. The trouble was that he would get his stories confused a lot, especially when he got into his cups.

Before the official engagement, actually before we even knew an engagement was a possibility, Daddy took The Widow to visit Uncle Elmore and Aunt Clara. I guess he wanted their approval and encouragement. Everyone was so worried about Daddy after Mama died that they were delighted that Daddy had a chance for happiness. Before the trip, Daddy told Bessie that they were going, but for her not to tell anyone. She didn't, not even her sister-in-law, Lorraine. Well, it seems The Widow could not keep such a secret. She called her friend from the church circle that called Daddy's neighbor Sudie Bea, the town crier. Sudie Bea, The Widow's distant kin, called everyone she could think of. Verda Lee said that she must have made 35 calls that morning, including the one she made to them.

Verda Lee and Sam had invited Daddy and The Widow to supper the night before the little trip. Our families went way back. One of the reasons Daddy decided to settle in Kingston to practice was its good quail hunting, dove hunting, duck hunting and fishing. Sam was the local vet. In another time, I believe that Verda Lee would have been a super-successful professional woman of some sort, but she grew up in the South at a time and in an era where a woman's success was measured by how well she married and what kind of house she ran. She was independent, efficient, and smart.

Mama envied few people, but Verda Lee was one of them. I think she was jealous of her independence and confidence, and the fact that she knew more about Daddy's business than Mama did. Sam had children about the same ages as Buchanan, Bessie and I. They felt a little betrayed and hurt when they found that the secret had been hidden from them, two of his best friends, only to be announced to the whole town, via Bertha, The Widow's church circle friend, and Sudie Bea.

When Daddy got home from Beaufort, he immediately found that the news of trip with The Widow was all over town. He accused Bessie of spreading the news. Bessie had not told. In fact, Lorraine, Bessie's sister-in-law, was a little hurt when someone called to ask her and she didn't already know. Of course, Bessie had kept Daddy's confidence. The Widow had not. But, did she admit it to Daddy? No, she let Bessie take the blame. Later, Verda Lee told Daddy how they all found out; The Widow had to admit that she indeed had told someone.

At this point, I need to say that when Daddy blames someone for something, it is never done politely or tactfully. He can be very blunt, unforgiving and sure of himself. He never apologized to Bessie. Neither did The Widow. The Widow was aware of the situation; the battle line was being drawn.

CHAPTER 10
"Diamonds are a girl's best friend."
Marilyn Monroe

Then there was THE RING. We had all already discussed what to do with THE RING. It, as a matter of fact, was the topic of discussion in the car on the way to Mama's funeral. That sounds rather a crass and materialistic topic, but we were all struggling for composure. When Daddy brought up this business-like concrete topic, it seemed a suitable distraction to keep us from having to deal with the real emotions we were experiencing. Heaven forbid that we show how we really felt! I remember at the funeral Anna Bet was about sixteen. She sat quietly sobbing. I envied her. I wanted to cry but I couldn't, not in public.

Later we thought we had decided, that since the ring had been a family heirloom, it should stay in the Bethea family. We thought that Daddy was going to give the ring to Buchanan, who would eventually give it to, his son, Buchanan R. or "Buchanan the Great" as he preferred to be called at the time, to give to his wife someday.

We called him Baby Buchanan for a long time but he wasn't very old before he rebelled at that name. "Buchanan the Great" acquired his name one Christmas. He was pretty young, but opened an electric shaver that The Widow had wrapped for Daddy. Buchanan was on the package. Parents often give children things sooner than they are ready for them but this was way premature. Daddy was John Buchanan Bethea, Jr., my brother was John Buchanan Bethea, III; and my nephew was Buchanan Rhatert Bethea. The only problem was that they all went by Buchanan. When my brother was growing up he was Little Buchanan and Daddy was Big Buchanan. That became confusing though when Little Buchanan grew taller than Big Buchanan. The situation was nearly impossible when Buchanan R. came along. When we were discussing how to differentiate, my young nephew suggested "Buchanan the Great". That worked!

Did Daddy give the ring to Buchanan? Oh, no! Daddy gave it to HER as an engagement ring. Personally, I wouldn't have wanted to wear my second husband's first wife's ring, but there is no accounting for greed. Justifying this, Daddy said that he couldn't be sure what kind of woman Buchanan R. would marry. "He might marry some slut", he said. That's why he said he went ahead and gave The Widow the ring.

Bessie just said, "Huh!" in a tone of voice that suggested, "Who's to say it's not already in such hands?" It didn't hold water with me either. It was just another forewarning. We had to keep telling ourselves that it is technically and legally his, and he can give it to whomever he wants-----but it somehow seemed immoral to us. Grand Mama, who thought the sun rose and set with Buchanan, would have been upset, I am sure. As for us, we were furious.

Later, The Widow flaunted the big ring. I think at first Mama's friends assumed that Daddy had simply bought her an unusually large diamond. Gradually, folks realized that she had THE RING. It created quite a stir.

After Daddy had given her THE RING they told us that they had decided not to tell anyone in town of the engagement, including Buchanan, Bessie and me until she had told all of her children. As we found later, she does not communicate as we do, casually. She likes big dramatic announcements. She was going to announce it to them, all at once at an upcoming big family gathering.

To keep the big secret, she wore THE RING around her neck on a gold chain like the ghost Alice of the Hermitage, the local Murrell's Inlet legend. This, however, was not the Old South. There was no irate father to hide from.

The big family gathering was yet a day off. Again, The Widow could not wait. She just had to sneak and show it off, delicately lifting the ring on its chain for a viewing. This time Bessie was in for the big surprise. When she and her family returned from vacation, there were about 20 messages on her answering machine. That's how she learned of Daddy's engagement. Verda Lee and Sam had invited Daddy and The Widow to dinner after she had the ring. Again, they didn't even tell their good friends. They were hurt like we were when they found the whole town knew, but they didn't.

Daddy did not tell Jannie Mae either. Mama and Jannie Mae had a unique relationship. Mama called Jannie Mae her "help". Jannie Mae told us Mama was her "eyeballs". Jannie Mae and her sister started coming in from Bucksport to Mama's one day a week to blitz clean. Mama was not really into housekeeping, but she wanted everything relatively clean. She didn't mind clutter, but hated dirt. She would not have Venetian blinds because they collected dust. She spent most of her time in the kitchen, visiting, and on her crafts.

In contrast, The Widow had Venetian blinds in all the bedrooms in the house even before the wedding. Mama kept the cabinets, drawers, and closets neat, but the rooms would often look as if a tornado had gone through them. Surface neatness was not her thing, so Jannie Mae and her sister would come in once a week and clean and straighten up. This was long before the days of professional cleaning services, but I would be willing to bet that there are, today, few professionals that could touch them for efficiency.

She paid them handsomely. This was probably Mama's one extravagance. Gradually, Mama and Jannie Mae had a routine worked out so that Mama knew exactly how to do things to suit Jannie Mae. She told me that before anyone else knew that Mama was sick, she did. She said that's why she started coming by more often

to help Mama. Sometimes she would come in after she had been to Mrs.
Bailey or after she had come in from her job at Myrtle Beach or "on
the beach" as she worded it.

Most of the labor pool of Myrtle Beach in those days was inland
folk. Jobs in our county were often hard to find. They would carpool
or ride a bus service, usually a dilapidated, converted school bus to the
beach in the morning, and return in the evening. Because Jannie Mae
was industrious, she owned her own automobile, which increased her
status and mobility considerably.

She also helped Ernestine, who married into the Bailey family,
one of those industrious, founding-father sorts of families every small
town seems to have. She lives in one of the few old Victorian homes
in Kingston, just off Kingston Lake, which feeds into the Waccamaw
River. Ernestine says she spends more thought on what to give Jannie
Mae for Christmas some years than she does on her own children.

Jannie Mae was invaluable to Mama during her illness. That's
when she began working for her full-time. Jannie Mae would rub her
back and her abdomen to make her more comfortable. It was as if
they needed no words to communicate during the last days of Mama's
illness. Mama asked Jannie Mae to promise to stay on and look after
Daddy until he got settled. Mama told Jannie Mae she hoped
Daddy would find someone else to marry. She felt that Daddy
would not be able to cope alone. She was right. That, I suppose,
is another reason we all tried to support Daddy's decision to
remarry.

Mama's illness was short, I suppose, as terminal illnesses
go. My husband's Mama died in June, just before Mama's
cancer was diagnosed. Mama left us the following June, several
months before their 42nd wedding anniversary. By the next
June The Widow was seriously courting Daddy.

Typically, Mama dismissed her aches and pains as
insignificant. So did her doctor, Daddy's cousin Montgomery.

I suppose everyone was so focused on her heart that her cancer was over looked. By the time it was diagnosed, there was little that could be done.

No one ever told me where her cancer started but I suspect that she, like Daddy, had lung cancer, but unlike Daddy's, hers was not curable. She had smoked Lucky Strike unfiltered cigarettes for years prior to her heart problems. She would often light a cigarette, forget about it and it would fall out of the ashtray and burn the window sill by the kitchen sink, or a side table. I have one "distressed" table that she helped distress. By the time Mama's cancer was discovered, it had spread.

Mama endured chemotherapy, radiation, loss of her hair; and sickening bouts of nausea, but to no avail. She finally decided to quit all treatment. By then she was pretty much bedridden and in a lot of pain. Between the Hospice nurses, Jannie Mae, Buchanan and Bessie, she had pretty good care. Unfortunately, I was living and working in Clemson at the time and wasn't near the help I wished I could have been. I called her every day and came home when I could.

As Mama became less and less able to get about, she moved out of the bedroom into the living room. Jannie Mae set up the old brass bed of mine from Aunt Daisy's, my Grand Mama's aunt, and Mama held court. She loved having visitors and seemed to feel best when someone was there. Fortunately, she had lots of visitors. Kitty, her best friend, did not come much though. She could not handle illness or unpleasantness, but Mama understood.

I always felt like Daddy should have been the one to move out of the bedroom. It was mighty inconvenient for Mama to have to walk down the hall to the bathroom.

As was usual with Mama, Daddy's needs were more important than hers. He still thought so, too. As the pain caused Mama more and more sleepless nights, it seemed to me that Daddy was more concerned with his own sleep being disturbed than her pain. I really resented that! Mama refused to take morphine for the pain because she was worried about becoming addicted. I thought to myself, "I'd rather deal with addiction in my last days than that much pain". When Mama asked me directly what I thought about her decision to stop chemotherapy, I didn't know what to say. I felt helpless and I knew the treatments were not working. All I could say was a tearful, "I can't stand to see you in so much pain."

During my last visit, although I knew the end was near, I needed to get back to Clemson so that BJ, my son, could get off to Boy Scout Camp. I hoped I could get back to Kingston in time, but I didn't. Mama and I had said good-bye but I still wished I could have gotten back. I was told that the day she died her friend Mary told Dr. Montgomery that Mama had to have help with the pain. When she died, Bessie had just left. Buchanan was with her, in the living room of Mama's house. Daddy was in their bedroom working a crossword puzzle.

CHAPTER 12
"Born to Lose" Ray Charles/Daddy

Needless to say, Jannie Mae's feelings were also really hurt when Betsy Rose came over and asked Jannie Mae if the story of Daddy's engagement were true. *Betsy Rose, another neighbor, and a member of Mama's bridge club, always kept tabs on what was going on at our house, or anywhere else for that matter. For example, one time when we were young and Mama and Daddy were not in town, some friends of mine and I decided to sun bathe on the roof. Betsy Rose came bustling right over and told us to get off that roof before we broke our necks. Of course, she also told Mama later.*

She always told everything. I wished I had a neighbor like that to watch my children so closely when I was raising them. When we were courting, Mama never allowed us to go in the house with our dates alone, but we could sit out in the yard chairs, if for any reason she and Daddy were both gone. She felt we should not give our neighbors reason to talk. It seems rather fitting and normal that Betsy Rose should be the one to tell Jannie Mae.

Betsy Rose, in her later years, also put her family in an uncomfortable position. She had a courtship with a 19-year-old boy/ man when she was in her eighties. They met at the retirement village where he worked as an orderly. This suitor was in love with another who was planning to have a sex-change operation. In the meantime he worked as a showgirl in one of the local "Gentleman's Clubs" at the beach. When the boyfriend learned that he could not get hold of her assets, even by marriage, he solemnly, without even a crack of a smile, tale her family that he could not go against their wishes and marry. He would have to be content with what he could get from her social security check. I think they cancelled their planned trip for Betsy Rose to meet his grandmother, twenty years her junior, because the courted was having trouble with her arthritis. What happens to folks when they get old? Loneliness must play most terrible tricks on their minds. In all other ways, Betsy Rose was as lucid as a fox. I think I'd rather deal with a casserole widow than a gold digging young stud.

In the whole situation, Bessie seemed to become the scapegoat. Daddy had those "Born to Lose" pity parties quite often to manipulate people into doing what he wanted. He liked to make people think he was deprived, the hardest worker, the most unappreciated, and the most generous, look-what-I-have-done-for-you-and-this-is-how-you-treat-me person in the whole town. He may have actually believed it himself. When Mama was sick and after she died, every day for almost a year and a half, Bessie would go by or call to make sure he had supper. She would go by after teaching school all day and fix supper for him, usually just something light, before she even went home herself.

Daddy told a tale of woe about never having anything to eat at the drugstore. One day, Mrs. Noble called Bessie.

"Bessie, I just thought I needed to call and let you know how concerned we are about your Daddy," informed Mrs. Noble.

"What's the matter?" responded Bessie anxiously.

"Did you know that your Daddy is not eating?' He says that he is so lonely he just doesn't feel like fixing supper and then eating alone. We are very concerned about him. We just felt like you needed to be aware of the situation," tattled Mrs. Noble

Bessie, completely disarmed, patiently explained, "I go by Daddy's every night to see that he has supper. Sometimes I bring him what we are eating, sometimes I fix a sandwich, or sometimes we pick up a take-out from Bubba's. I always ask what he prefers. I assure you, he is NOT doing without supper, unless by choice."

Bessie was furious and embarrassed. She was not neglecting her daughterly duties and she couldn't believe that Daddy was publicly implying she would. This, however, was mild compared to what was yet to come.

Another of Daddy's favorite tales of woe was that his friends had deserted him after Mama died. I realize that the relationship changes between friends when a person is no longer part of a couple, but his accusations were incredulous. He would claim no one came to see him. His friends would come by, but if more than two wound up in his den talking, he might just disappear into his bedroom to do his crossword puzzles. Or worse yet, he might have his bullbats, as he called his evening drink, get into his pajamas and go to bed, leaving them sitting up in the den. In fact, on the night of Mama's funeral, he did that very thing, and had no idea who had come by to offer condolences. Many of these folks had come some distance to be there, too. It was not unusual for him to go to bed hours before dark, in the summertime. If he began his bullbats at five, which he usually did, he was actually quite rude. He wondered why friends quit coming by.

Often people would invite him out, he would accept, and then back out at the last minute. Sam said that he did it over and over when they had a fishing trip planned. Sam would work to get everything ready to go, and if you know anything about fishing, you know that it is quite a ritual. He would go to pick Daddy up. Daddy would back out. He always had some excuse. Daddy was just not able to accept the friendly gestures of his friends. It amazed me the great lengths to which people went to try to include him. I don't believe that he was deserted, but that he was the one who failed to cultivate his old friendships.

CHAPTER 13
Murphy's Law

Buchanan and I began to join Bessie in the realization that all was not well the night of the dinner. The Widow invited Bessie and Lou, Buchanan and JoNelle, Scott and me to dinner. Scott had not come to Kingston with me on that particular trip. The children were not included in this little get-together, which in our family was most unusual. We used to bemoan the fact that we could hardly finish a conversation without some childhood catastrophe intervening.

One such day, probably our worst, was one weekend the spring after Mama died. The aunts and uncles and all the cousins gathered at Daddy's for our usual everybody-bring-something family meal. My family was staying at Daddy's. When JoNelle and Buchanan got there, the youngest, Sarah Beth, still a baby, had taken to walking only on her tiptoes. Dr. Palmer came over and checked her out. Anna Bet, the oldest and now a teen-ager, came downstairs overly concerned about an emerging pimple on her chin. When Bessie and her family arrived Lori had Grand look at her infected thumb. He did so with great care. After lunch the children went outside for a kickball game in the side yard. A wasp stung Buchanan R., when he was playing under a fig tree. He is highly allergic. An epinephrine shot was in order. BJ got hot and sweaty and broke out in a rash all over his neck and chest. We put cream on it. He returned to the game. When it was his turn, he gave the ball a solid whack, Leslie reached out to stop it, it hit her arm, and she heard her arm snap. She came in and announced calmly, "I broke my arm." Sure enough, a trip to the hospital confirmed it.

She recognized a break because it was the third time she had broken her arm. Bessie said she was afraid the surgeon was going to think she and Lou abused the child! Later that afternoon Buchanan R. went to visit a friend and scratched the cornea of his eye.

As my family loaded the car to leave, Belle began throwing up. Another trip to the drugstore was in order. What a day! The only unscathed grandchild was Mary Ann. We really had a hard time finishing any conversation that day! I wonder if Mary Ann felt left out or lucky?

CHAPTER 14

"May I have your attention, please?" The Widow

At the time I thought the invitation to dinner was a friendly gesture, but I have since realized that it was a calculated move. Belle and I had been out to The Widow's condo once before on another visit. I was very ill at ease because I was afraid she would spill something. Here we were on a concrete patio, overlooking the golf course drinking hot chocolate out of her best china cups. I suppose that it is better than sitting on the best furniture on the best carpet inside drinking hot chocolate out of the good china cups. Daddy raved and raved about how peaceful it was out there. I felt anything but peaceful. I just knew Belle, who was only about five, then was going to drop that cup. Already I felt the attitude, that children could be a great bother.

The Widow had a condo on the golf course. She supposedly left the family farm, bought this condo and a white Thunderbird, and set out to catch a rich man.

It wasn't peaceful the night we went to dinner, either. She had invited Bessie, Buchanan and me, and our spouses, and, of course, Daddy for dinner. Dinner, not supper! Lou and JoNelle were there, but Scott was not able to come.

When we first arrived, we were all a little nervous, especially when she served lemonade out of dainty crystal stemware from a silver tray. It felt like a circle meeting of the ladies at the church. I can still see the expression on Lou's face as he held that dainty glass. He likes things plain and simple and putting on airs is unheard of for him. He works for the Department of Social Services and he knows what is real and what is superficial. He grew up in a family that cared for one another and lived a relatively simple, hard-working life. His father was a vocational teacher and on the side was caretaker for the Riverside Club. His mother stayed home to look after her aging mother and an invalid uncle who had become disabled after a bout with Rocky Mountain spotted fever as a child. Later when Lou's father died of lung cancer I think he really resented the time he and Bessie spent looking after Daddy when he could have spent more time with his own father.

Anyway, we fixed our plates and began to eat, after a very ceremonious blessing. Blessings at our house usually consisted of "Thank the Lord for supper" except on Thanksgiving or Christmas when we had the longer "Lord make us Thankful for these and all our many blessings." The things we were thankful for were named. Petitions were delivered. It ended with "Lord bless this food we are about to eat and us to thy service. Amen." Hers was much longer.

The food was not the best. The roast beef was dry and we had broccoli. Roast was Mama's specialty and she usually cooked it using a meat thermometer and keeping a watchful eye on it, basting it regularly. She used to say, "You can't rush good cooking." Daddy never liked broccoli. The Widow commented that she was sure he would like "hers." I remember thinking; a rose by any other name is still a rose. He still didn't like it, but he politely tried some. It seemed he could find his manners when it suited him.

We were beginning to relax and enjoy ourselves, when she suddenly picked up her water glass and tapped it loudly with her silver-plated fork. She proceeded to give us a "this-is-how-it-is-going-to-be talk." It started off all sweet-like. Something about how she could never take Mama's place in our lives.

"I just wanted to let you children know how fortunate I feel to be marrying your father. I never expected to find such happiness. I know that I could never take your mother's place in your lives, but I will try to make your father happy."

She continued, "Your father and I have decided that it would be best if I moved into his house. He feels he'd be cramped in this small condo and doesn't want to leave his home."

"So far, so good," I thought. We waited silently for her to continue.

She went on, "I, of course will want to make some changes, so it will become my home, too."

"Okay, that is reasonable. I would want to make some changes, too, if it were me."

"You know I have four children. I hope your daddy's home will become home for them, too."

"That could be a lot of fun," I thought hopefully.

Then came the bombshell. "I want you to all know you are welcome to visit, within reason."

"What?!!!!! Visit?!!! You don't visit home, you go home. What is within reason?"

Buchanan found his tongue first. He politely and smoothly responded, "We welcome you to our family and hope you and Daddy will be very happy."

Mama and Daddy had always had an open-door policy. Now we were told that we could visit, "within reason". We got the message. I'm not sure Daddy heard her though.

Later, when I asked Daddy about what they, for I guessed by now she was doing his talking for him, meant by "within reason", he didn't even remember the remark. He asked her about it and she said that she was talking about her out of town children, not us. Did Daddy buy that? Yes! Did I? No! Besides that, if she felt the need to limit her own children's visits, how would you expect her to feel about ours?

Now up until this time, Bessie was the only one who really expressed any real reservations about the marriage, but this little dinner party got to Buchanan and me, too. The more we thought about it the madder we got. We were so shocked at the time that none of us said a word. Of course, later we thought of all those clever, horrible things that we should have said. Sometimes I regret that Scott was not there that night because he probably would have said something, then and there. But of course, then I would have been embarrassed. And we probably would have had a gigantic fight over it. At least though, maybe we would have shown some backbone. In retrospect, I felt that The Widow knew that Buchanan, Bessie and I could not handle confrontation and that we were easy marks. (It was not easy bucking Daddy in any way. Mama taught us that, too.)

CHAPTER 15
"All's fair in love and war and babysitters." Evelyn

Although we weren't much for open warfare, we did begin to see that there might be some things we may have to fight for, if not with open warfare, then with guerrilla tactics. Our first skirmish was over the china. To us, china represents more than just china. Somehow family values and traditions are represented by china. I know it sounds silly and I can't quite explain it but that's how it is. It seems Daddy and The Widow decided that we could go ahead and get Mama's china, except for the Billingsly Rose and the Christmas China. Keep in mind now, at this point, Bessie is the only one who has expressed real reservations about the whole affair.

Mama had promised Bessie the Billingsly Rose china. In fact she had given Bessie part of the set already. It was displayed in her china cabinet in her dining room. Knowing The Widow, like I do now, I agree with Bessie that she may have noticed that china in her house. Looks like she would have been aware enough to realize that if she wanted peace in the family she ought to shy away from that particular set of china. But no, that's definitely not her style. In Mama's dining room china cabinet, there were three sets of good china. On the top shelf was Grand Mama's French Haviland. I have a set of Haviland china that I chose because I loved Grand Mama's so. That was obviously for me, on the second shelf was the Billingsly Rose, Bessie's, and on the bottom was the quail china, Buchanan's, who loves hunting, fishing and the outdoors. There was also the Christmas china in the attic; a set of twenty-four, ready to be divided into three sets of eight, obviously.

At this particular time, I probably had more china than Bessie or Buchanan because I got married the first time just before the china and silver prices shot out of sight. I had a big wedding, though not as big as Daddy's. Because of Mama and Daddy's standing in the community, I had all the china I could ever really hope to use. I also had finished out my Haviland pattern by buying some pieces from Betsy Rose's son, when he was closing it out of his jewelry store.

Well, when Daddy announced that we could get the china in the dining room, except for the Billingsly Rose, it hit the fan with Bessie. After that little power play on the part of The Widow, I decided that this was the time to go ahead and explain to Daddy how it might be better for them to use the Haviland and give Bessie the Billingsly Rose. He agreed, and that was that, I thought. Later, when The Widow was visiting, Daddy told Bessie, like she was a young child who had just been given a new pair of socks by a maiden aunt, "Thank The Widow for the china." I thought Bessie would choke, but Bessie looked at her and squeaked, "Thank you," in not an exactly thankful tone, but still said the words. Lou said he wished that she had refused to say that, but again she was so shocked that her training of obedience and good manners overpowered her fury.

At first, The Widow had decided to keep the Christmas china. After returning home to Greenwood after that particular trip when the china incident had occurred, I called Bessie and we decided we ought to push for the Christmas china, too. This was war. We knew it now, but we felt like Confederates fighting what we knew was a losing battle against a powerful, well-trained, better-equipped Yankee army. We were not surrendering yet, though, Bessie told Daddy I wanted the Christmas china. Tit-for-tat, I suppose. He let us have it. We gave Jannie Mae a set of four, I took a set of eight, and Bessie and Buchanan took place settings of six each.

Possibly, in retaliation, I don't really know, The Widow's children gave her a very expensive set of china as a wedding gift. I know it was very expensive, because I started to buy them some Christmas mugs in their pattern for Christmas one year, and they were in a price range that I considered conspicuous consumption. Much later, in an off-hand, casual way, The Widow told me that Grand Mama's old china was somewhere out in the attic in the garage and I could get it if I wanted it. I did want it, so I hurriedly retrieved it before he could change his mind.

Scott said that the last thing in the world we needed was any more china at our house. He said that one-day when I came in from a summer sale on Christmas china with two serving bowls for our inexpensive Christmas china that Kaye had given us. I expect he may be right, but instead of admitting it, I defended it by saying, "I'll stop bringing china into the house when you stop buying so much fishing stuff." After all, I need to have enough china for five to fight over. Scott and I have five children: his, mine, and ours. I had two, he had two, and we have one. By the way, guess what Daddy and The Widow gave Anna Bet when she married? China, of course.

Anna Bet's wedding did not follow quite the traditional way, but it worked out. The only real hitch was when BJ wandered in through the dining room door right in the middle of the exchanging of the vows. She told me on Wednesday that she was getting married to Allen on Saturday. I sat down on the kitchen chair, stunned. My stepdaughter was getting married in a month or so and we had spent almost a year preparing. Now we had three days. By Saturday afternoon, though, we put on a nice, quiet little family wedding in the living room. My friend Beverly furnished the flowers and Bessie and I scrounged around and managed a respectable showing, including a cake. I have yet to go to a wedding where I thought the bride's flowers were more beautiful. Bessie, Lou, Lori and Leslie came, so did Buchanan's family. Amazingly, so did Daddy and The Widow. I was glad.

The china leads into another interesting situation. When Daddy asked us to get the living room furniture, he also told us that The Widow did not want to use the custom made cherry harvest table in the den. This was another ominous sign. This was where the grandchildren ate Thanksgiving and Christmas dinner or any other meal when there was a family gathering. She also had the bar taken out of the kitchen where we had always eaten informal meals. It sat six. She replaced it with a table for two. When I first saw that table with its two little fancy lace placemats and two chairs only, I got the message loud and clear. NO MORE BIG INFORMAL FAMILY GATHERINGS HERE. From then on, everything would be formal invitation only.

In the years that they were married, I ate very few meals at my Daddy's home. One Christmas when we couldn't think of what to give The Widow for Christmas, Lori suggested that maybe a good cookbook would be the thing. I personally believe that it was not a matter of not knowing how, but rather a matter of not wanting to cook for US. Once, when I was visiting town for the weekend, Daddy didn't have time to come eat with US because they were planning a big get together, a meal for THEM, and her children. I would be lying if I said that didn't hurt my feelings.

It seemed to me that it was during the three-month

engagement period, that The Widow and Bessie found it harder to hide the fact that they were at odds. The weekend I went to get my share of the furniture, we planned the rehearsal party. Daddy had asked us early in the engagement if we wanted to go in with her children to give them a reception after what was supposedly going to be a small, intimate wedding with family and close friends. Since it was traditional for the family of the groom to give a "rehearsal" party for family and out of town guests we offered to do that instead. Daddy had said that he would enjoy something like this. We thought that this would be a great opportunity to get to know her children better. Boy, were we naïve! For one thing, we have learned that small and informal was not a part of The Widow's vocabulary. I heard one of her daughters say later that when she found out her mother was coming to visit a sick granddaughter, she hired a cleaning service to come clean, and ordered the meat tray from the deli, just to have sandwiches. One Thanksgiving after Daddy and The Widow were married, one of her daughters brought a dish leftover from her in-law's family meal. There was plenty left to share. The Widow refused to use it because it couldn't be properly served in a silver-serving dish. Now I'm not knocking formal dinners. They can be quite elegant and fun, but as Mama used to say, "There is a time and a place for everything."

CHAPTER 16
"Man's best friend is his dog." Tom

N ow the months prior to the wedding were increasingly tense. To start with there was the question of the location and size of the wedding. We assumed that it would be, as Daddy had said, just family and closest friends, therefore, small. There was a big discussion about "the list" early on in the proceedings. The Widow first suggested that Bessie (poor, old Bessie) do the list for Daddy's side. By now we were becoming more and more familiar with her modus operandi. Bessie realized that this would for sure make her the scapegoat if someone were not included. The Widow could just say, "Well, Bessie made the list." Bessie wisely bowed out of that. Later Edna Earle, our former next-door neighbor and one of Mama's bridge club friends, suggested that Daddy consider using his Christmas list as a guide. That's what he eventually tried to do. Now if The Widow had just limited hers to her Christmas CARD list maybe things would not have gotten so out of hand.

Anyway, it was settled that the wedding would be in the big church at 3:00 PM on the Saturday after Thanksgiving. Even the preacher had privately suggested to Lou that we try to talk them into something more discreet when he caught wind of the plans. Lou knew better than to even think about trying to say something to them. That the preacher would think that Lou could have talked to them showed that those outside our family and most of Mama's friends had no idea of the struggle we were in. To an outsider, especially the preacher, this seemed to be a great match.

Mama had not been a big church-going person, though she had a very strong faith. She used to hate to go to church when all she could hear was "Where's Dr. Buchanan?" There were some who acted like he was THE great doctor himself, and I think Mama just got sick of all the adoration he got and that she had to listen to, especially knowing he was often out fishing or hunting, not really working, as he often liked others to believe.

Besides, Mama had a big resentment about how they came to be members of the First Methodist Church in Kingston. Now Grand Mama Bethea was a Baptist, who married a Methodist and became a Methodist. Grand Mama Rhatert was a Presbyterian who married a Lutheran. Daddy was Methodist and Mama was Presbyterian. I think she assumed that they would visit around and decide together what church to join in Kingston. Well, Daddy up and joined the Methodist Church for both of them one weekend when Mama was in Charleston visiting Granddaddy and Kaye. This did not sit well with Mama, especially since Daddy was often called away and worked on Sundays, and it would be up to Mama to get us all there, by herself, and attend without him. I still don't feel comfortable attending church alone. It is such a "family" place. A church can be a lonely place. I especially felt that way when I was a single mom.

When someone needed Mama, especially her friends, she was always there, even in situations where others found it too uncomfortable to be. She had a beautiful faith and spirituality that I have come to appreciate more and more as I get older. It used to bother me that she wasn't more like the little old ladies of the church. Now I am proud of just who she was. Mama didn't need the church to organize her good works.

Now Daddy was marrying someone who had brought

him back to the fold. Daddy was now, in his own words, a "dues paying Methodist" again. Most preachers do like the dues paying kind to come back into the flock.

Just before Tom died, Harriette told me that Tom asked Daddy if he knew how to pray. Daddy sort of sputtered, Harriette said. I know Mama knew how to pray. I think Daddy might have. I'm not sure he listened though.

Tom, Kitty's husband, asked Daddy right before he was getting married why he wanted to do such a thing. Daddy said that he was lonely. Tom said, "Get a dog, Buck, get a dog". Tom knew how to get to the heart of an issue. Daddy didn't listen.

I know now, there were those who were worried about Mama's salvation. She didn't even have her own preacher to conduct her funeral. Dr. Lovette, the Baptist Minister who visited Mama often when she was dying, spoke at her funeral. It was held at the funeral home, not at the church. Daddy had a big funeral at the church; so will The Widow. I go to church today. So do Bessie and Buchanan, but I want to spend my eternity with Mama's God!

CHAPTER 17
"It's better to under dress than to overdress."
Mama

Back to the church wedding! It seems that The Widow ran away to Dillon for her first marriage. They say that she ran off with her sister's fiancé. Dillon is a little town just across from the North Carolina border where out of state folks would come to take advantage of South Carolina's loose marriage requirements. I always thought it was a rather seedy, tacky place. To some, the magistrate's office there was called a wedding chapel. To others, it was called a marriage-mill. This time The Widow wanted to have a real church wedding, and a real church wedding it would be.

It was beginning to feel more like a sideshow now than a wedding. We realized it would call for more formal attire than just "church clothes". When I asked The Widow what she was going to wear, she said that she would just be wearing a little off-white suit that she was making herself. Ha! By now we knew that she did not always tell things exactly as they were going to be. We knew we'd better shop for something to wear that you could dress up or down, depending on what the situation called for when we got there. Bessie, JoNelle and I were back and forth on the phone many, many times, discussing various possibilities until we were satisfied with our families' wardrobes. We wanted to make Mama proud. We wanted to look prosperous, but not over done. But we knew we had to do more than our usual L. L. Bean type everyday clothes and schoolteacher's jumpers. We all seriously considered dressing in mourners black for the occasion, but discarded the idea when we thought about how it would reflect on our upbringing. Of course, since then black has become acceptable wedding attire. We were taught though that it was not appropriate to wear black or white to a wedding unless of course you were the bride, in a first marriage.

Now for the small, informal rehearsal supper ... we asked for the list about three weeks before the wedding. Boy, did we get it. Daddy had asked eight couples. She had twenty-seven, including their children, if any. This put a whole new light on our plans. We scrapped intimate oyster roast/seafood buffet and opted for the traditional buffet type food. Since it was still early in the cool weather, "R" months, that many really good fresh oysters could be a problem. We batted ideas back and forth, including serving informal game dishes, but decided that we would try to be accommodating and do what the bride seemed to want, a more formal to-do. We would have a drop-in buffet, with heavy hors d'oeuvres.

There was controversy about the time. We knew it would have to be fairly early or else Daddy would get into his bullbats and may not even come. He might just go to bed with everybody there, like he's done many a time before. Like he did at Mama's visitation the night before her funeral. People excused his behavior as that of the grief stricken widower. We settled on six-thirty. I brought the invitations back to Greenwood to do. I did not have all the addresses. I had a time finding them. I ended up having to call Lenna Mae and Charlie, which I felt was rather tacky, but Daddy could not or would not give me the addresses. Lenna Mae was Daddy's old girlfriend who later married his friend from medical school,

Charlie. Daddy said he was writing a letter to Lenna Mae when he heard that the Japanese had attacked Pearl Harbor.

Bessie and JoNelle were stuck with the rest of the arrangements. They assigned me punch. Of course, it was to be Methodist punch, which I felt was rather hypocritical, since everybody knew Daddy wouldn't do without. What happened, of course, were those who wanted stronger spirits just sneaked out to their cars to get what they wanted. How tacky! I personally would have preferred to set up an honest bar. It seems rather silly to pretend there will be no drinking. I think The Widow thought that once she married Daddy then he would be rescued from the misery that caused him to drink so heavily and that he would quit. She would save him. (I don't have to even tell how that turned out.)

One of Daddy's favorite party foods was cheese biscuits with pineapple preserves, so that was to be one item on the menu. *Rosa used to make them for us. Rosa Lee was Mama's help that raised Bessie, loved Buchanan to death, and would always listen to my pre-adolescent problems when I came home from school. She came early in the mornings, did the washing and ironing, cleaning, and although Mama was an excellent cook, Rosa did most of the cooking. She would cook things like homemade biscuits, apple pie, and the best fried chicken, rice and gravy that you ever put in your mouth. She had an unmarried, promiscuous daughter who had five children, most of whom did not have the same father, and Rosa was trying to help raise them. Later in the consciousness-raising era of the sixties, I wondered how in the world she managed. I remember her singing "What a Friend We Have In Jesus" all the time. I liked Rosa's God, too. He had to be real to get her through life without bitterness and despair.*

Rosa Lee was too old now for so much cooking, so we asked Lenna to do it. *Lenna worked for the Riverside Club. The Riverside Club was a supper club that Mama and Daddy's friends put together when they were young. At that time, in Kingston there were no golf courses or clubhouses for socializing. Most of them had small children at the time, and they felt like they needed a place to get away. At that time there were only two country clubs at Myrtle Beach, and the road to the beach was a single lane highway that became impossibly jammed with traffic in the summer. They rented an old house that Evelyn and Ed used to live in on the Waccamaw and the Riverside Club was established.*

I remember the planning and work Mama did when she was "on the committee" or when she "had the club supper." It later became much more organized and we had many parties. When we were freshmen in college, Harriette, Frankie, Jessie, and I hosted a party there for all our friends. Later, they started calling them debutante parties. That sort of thing never really took hold in Kingston. I think we were a little backwoods for that. Fortunately, that is a custom that has gone by the wayside. The land the club was later built on belonged to Kitty and Tom and at that time was probably worth very little. Every time there were big rains, the road would get flooded and they couldn't even get into the building, and Hurricane Floyd almost wiped it out. Today, land along the Waccamaw is a premium, as swampy and low as it is. But that area has some sort of water percolation problem that still makes it less valuable than some. I think the local Christian School is built on more of their land. Ironically, I heard that once a preacher in town did a sermon on how the Riverside club members were all in danger of eternal damnation but I don't think that particular preacher had ever been there. He thought it was a den of iniquity, I guess. It was probably easier to preach about this than those in his own congregation. JoNelle and Buchanan are members of the club today. Bessie, Buchanan, and I inherited from Daddy stock in the club that Buchanan says is essentially worthless. I guess The Widow didn't want it.

Bessie and JoNelle continued to work on the food for the

party. They ordered a honey-ham thinly sliced, and called the Downtown Café to do a vegetable tray and slice our roast beef. Wallace did the best job in town at the time we thought. We would fill in with the traditional dips, fruitcake, and fancy breads a fruit tray and a table of sweets, including Daddy's favorite, light fruitcake without raisins.

The fruit was an idea Bessie got from Alma at Nellie's Beauty Shop. When we were growing up Nellie's was the place to go to the beauty parlor. Mama would send me. She and Bessie had naturally curly hair, which I envied tremendously, still do. She had no idea how to fix mine that barely even had a wave and was as fine as corn silk. I remember Edna Earle and Frankie, our neighbors, had the tightest pin curls with the bobby pins making the neatest little X's. The pin curls covered their entire scalps. Rosa tried her hand at trying to roll mine in socks, but it was a failure. My pin curls were always rather straggly and hodge podge.

Bessie would cut the top of a pineapple and use it for a centerpiece on a silver tray. She would decorate it with toothpicks, cherries, kiwis and I don't know what all. It would look very elegant. JoNelle was in charge of the crab dip. We tried to plan for convenience. Something where we would not have to do a lot of cooking since Bessie and I were both teaching and I was living in Greenwood, 200 miles away, as well.

SHE put a quick stop to THAT. The day after I went back to Greenwood, thinking all was well. Buchanan, The Widow and Daddy were talking casually around at Daddy's. The subject of the menu for the party came up. Buchanan innocently told them what we were planning. I hear she pitched a royal fit. She got all hot and bothered and said that we couldn't possibly serve what we were planning because that was "exactly" what she was having at the reception. She said people would think she was serving leftovers. Buchanan told us we HAD to change the menu.

Now at this time Buchanan was a CPA, into working on a pre-nuptial agreement and was trying not to rock the boat too much. I don't need to say though that this did not go over too well with Bessie. We changed the menu. Buchanan had to agree to go to the beach and get shrimp and crab so that we could serve marinated shrimp in place of the roast beef. Bessie and JoNelle, with the help of Verda Lee, spent more time than they thought they had messing with that shrimp. You know, boiling, peeling, and cleaning shrimp is no piece of cake. Just storing that much shrimp to marinate creates problems. Let me tell you too, that there is quite a difference in the price of shrimp and the price of roast beef. We all had to dig deeper in our pockets to finance this affair than we had planned.

I was really beginning to resent this, the expense and trouble this wedding was turning out to be. By this point we were beginning to resent a lot of things. What made it worse was that we felt like we had to act like all was well or appear to be selfish, money-grubbing adult children standing in the way of our poor old widowed father's happiness.

So we went on with the party. Bessie and JoNelle rounded up a silver punch bowl and cups Edna Earle offered, as well as a large chaffing dish and coffee cups. They lined up a shrimp bowl from Verda Lee. Bessie's Sister-in-law offered to make a strawberry cheese ball.

Bessie and JoNelle made arrangements for the details like flowers, tablecloths, candles and napkins. On the day of the party, all we were to do was to set-up. Bessie was feeling more and more put-upon. I was out-of-town and that made more fall on her shoulders.

CHAPTER 17

"Don't throw more out of the back door than you bring in the front door." Mama

Let me back up and mention the pre-nuptial agreement again. I guess enough people, including Daddy's lawyer, had their doubts about The Widow's good intentions that it was decided that this agreement was in order. The deal was, according to what Daddy assured us early in the engagement, that everything she brought into the marriage would go to her children and everything Daddy had, would go to us.

Now let me tell you, I had to wonder if she already had very much if she had been so intent on getting Mama's china and silver and had to go out and buy new living room furniture. Many people advised us to go in and take everything we could get our hands on of Mama's before the wedding. They said that once she moved in we could kiss Mama's things good-bye. I wish I could say that they had been wrong.

Let me give you one example, a rather insignificant sounding, and small example. One Christmas, Bessie, JoNelle and I each cross-stitched a Charleston scene for Mama. She was originally from Charleston, which probably explains why she so often was frustrated with some of Kingston's small town ways. She had the handwork all matted and framed in one frame, which she hung over the mantle in the den. Shortly after the wedding, it was of course, replaced. We even understood why The Widow would want do to that. We got to wondering what she did with it, so I asked Daddy. He became very defensive and accused Bessie of being greedy and putting me up to asking him. How absurd! He said that it belonged to HIM and HE could do with it what he wanted. They hung it in the upstairs hall. I've always wondered if she hung it before or after I called and asked about it. This sounds very petty, but that picture represented more to us than an ornament for the house. His response to us was also hurtful.

To insure that Daddy's wishes would be honored, Buchanan felt that they needed to be in writing. For example, Daddy had said before that he planned to leave the house to Bessie and Lou since they had been such a help to him, and since Buchanan and I both already had as much of a house as we would probably ever want.

In retrospect, I figure all that maneuvering was a waste of time, and I doubt there was any mention of what was to be with things accumulated during their marriage, most of which would be purchased with Daddy's assets. I'm sure. Mama, in her later years, talked about how her kitchen had become obsolete and needed redoing. She always wanted oriental rugs. She prided herself in saving money by not going to the beauty parlor every week. She missed many an outing with her friends so that she could be home to fix lunch for Daddy. She had many of her clothes made when she felt clothes her size were too expensive in the department stores. She bought material at outlets to save money on curtains and draperies. She let them hang for decades before replacing them. I don't think Mama really understood what Daddy had. Even if she had, she came from a place and from an era where it was more acceptable to be poor, but proud, than to be new rich. The folks in Pawley's called it arrogantly shabby. New rich was too, close to carpet bagging, rather like a few people think of the snowbirds that regularly descend on the beach. When Mama would take me shopping as a teenager she would point out to me how many patients Daddy had to see in order to buy me an outfit. She was always the home economist.

We expected The Widow to make changes in the house. It did need sprucing up and I suppose no woman would feel altogether at home in her husband's first wife's home.(It didn't seem to bother her about the ring, though, did it, or about the silver?) She painted the whole house, inside and out, put on a new roof because she didn't like the color, replaced all the wallpaper, and redid the kitchen, TWICE, the second time replacing the beautiful, solid pine paneling with shiny dark cherry and new cabinets.

She should have done the same to the den because it really does look strange with the pine paneling in the den butting up against the cherry in the kitchen right at the door that most people use when they come in the house.

I expected the fish to go any day. In the den was a stuffed ninety-one pound blue marlin that Daddy caught in the Gulf Stream while fishing with Hub, another of his old Citadel friends. To tell you the truth the fish did dominate the den, and I would probably want to donate it to some seafood restaurant myself, but the fish became the last symbol of Daddy's manhood. If the fish went, we figured all hope would be gone. There was a plaque by the fish that told the date it was caught and reiterated that it was caught under duress. I gather that it took a great deal of encouragement from his fishing buddies to enable Daddy to land the fish in the first place.

In addition to redoing the kitchen, rugs, mostly oriental, grace every floor in the house, including the upstairs hallways. Gradually, the den had been changed from English Country, to early bawdyhouse. At first, Daddy had said she could do whatever she wanted to the rest of the house but the den was his. I guess she showed him. I think she waited until his bullbats and then got him to promise stuff. He couldn't remember what he did or he didn't say, he just went along with whatever she wanted.

Outside they built a new sprinkler system. The city had to replace the pipes leading into the whole neighborhood so that the system would work after it was installed. They've paved the quarter mile driveway with concrete and, would you believe, speed bumps. To drive on the driveway, in a matter of less than a dozen years, they bought three Lincoln Town Cars, one Cadillac, and two Blazers. They took one car back after just a few weeks and traded it. She didn't like it like she thought she would. Later, The Widow paid someone mega bucks to remove one of the speed bumps. It reminded me of prisoners on the rock piles digging a hole and then covering it up. I'm sure the only reason they didn't buy one of the more expensive foreign status-symbol cars was that Daddy had this thing about American made cars. He could be stubborn sometimes.

They weren't able to carry out her travel plans because Daddy was uncooperative about getting a passport. It's not the money he considered. He never did like to travel. Grand Mama was like that and unfortunately, so am I. Bessie and Buchanan love to travel.

The reason Daddy has money at all was not altogether his hard work, although he did work hard, nor his wise investments. Uncle Ellis, a bachelor uncle of Grand Mama's, invented a gadget that went on the cotton gin that made him a small fortune. The uncle invested it wisely. Some was left to Grand Mama. Grand Mama's portion of his estate left her very comfortably well off. She was so frugal with her share that she refused to redo her bathroom when it really needed it because she felt it was frivolous. Mama told me, too, that Pop, my grandfather on Daddy's side, never did like the idea that she had more money than he did. I guess that caused her to show some restraint, too. Grand Mama left half of her share to Daddy.

Buchanan had tried to look after Daddy and his grandchildren in this pre-nuptial agreement. It was an exercise in futility, though, because, as Mama the home economist always said, "Don't throw more out of the back door than you bring in the front door." The Widow and Daddy used a very wide back door.

This pre-nuptial agreement though, was being negotiated and of course, we had no way of predicting the future, so we meekly changed our plans for the rehearsal party and remained the smiling, dutiful daughters and daughter-in-law, at the insistence of Buchanan.

CHAPTER 18
"Never wear black or white to a wedding." Mama

The rehearsal party went well. The day of the party we ran around like chickens with our heads cut off, trying to get things done. Bessie's friend, Libby, came over, flitted around and added her artistic touch to the decorations, and we pulled it off fairly well. Of course, the bar opened in the driveway, much to The Widow's dismay. Bessie and I felt as if all her family were scrutinizing us the entire evening. Most of her family was much more overdressed than we were. Some of Mama and Daddy's out of town friends who came took the opportunity to let us know how wonderful they felt The Widow was for Daddy and for us to be sure to support the marriage. Thankfully, they thought the party was great and told us so. We smiled and nodded.

The next day was the wedding. The small informal, only close friends and family wedding. The blushing young bride was only sixty-seven and did not look a day over sixty. The groom was having great difficulty breathing. The weather was perfect. The church was decorated to the hilt with fresh flowers and candles, with acolytes to light the candles. The soft organ music drifted over the sanctuary as the guests took their seats. One daughter of the bride could hardly sit because of back trouble. It was questionable whether or not she would be able to attend at all.

The grandchildren were seated on the groom's side where

they could see clearly. A soloist sang. The groom and the preacher entered, with Buchanan serving as best man. The music got louder. "Here Comes the Bride" echoed through the sanctuary. The lights dimmed. All eyes turned expectantly to watch the blushing bride come down the aisle on the arm of her son. When I turned to look, instead of the blushing bride, here came Jannie Mae instead on the arm of a groomsman. We all scooted over to let her in the pew.

The wedding proceeded. This is the second-largest church in town, by the way. It probably seats at least six hundred. That was not a little homemade off white suit she was wearing, either. It was a floor-length, off-white gown that had these sparkly looking things all down the front. It reminded me of those Marilyn Monroe type sheath dresses, but of course The Widow did not have Marilyn's shape. I was so embarrassed. This was to be more of a spectacle than I had ever dreamed possible. We just kept smiling. During the ceremony, the preacher, one of The Widow's brothers, scanned us all with his sharp eyes stopped when he came to us, and said, "What God has joined together, let no man put asunder." I remember thinking; we waited too late to do anything about putting things asunder. Do you think God put this thing together?

Now we had to face the reception.

The reception was not what most people envision when they think of close family and friends. The First Methodist Church took up a whole block. On one corner was the Historic Hut Bible Class building. In the middle was the Fellowship Hall, a white Mission-styled Sanctuary with stained glass pictures in the windows. On the other corner was the Big White Church where the wedding took place. Each building was bigger than the previous one. After the wedding, as is the custom, the wedding party returned to the church for a few pictures, then proceeded through to the Fellowship Hall to form a receiving line to greet guests. The guests lined up to "speak" to the bride and groom, sample the food, and visit with other guests. There were the usual comments on the flowers, the music, and the dresses, the expressions on faces, the preacher, the attendees, and anything else anyone could think of to nit-pick. It was a beautiful, warm, Carolina blue-sky day, the Saturday after Thanksgiving. They scheduled the wedding around the Carolina/Clemson ballgame because many guests, including close family, would have definitely balked at coming, more than the normal balking of some about going to the wedding if they had not. The line of guests wound all around the block. I think everyone who got an invitation to the wedding and reception showed up. Only God and The Widow knew how many invitations were sent. I had to stand in line forty minutes to "speak" to my own Daddy. We were not included in the back-hall walk from the church to the fellowship hall. During my wait in line I stood by Kitty and some of Mama and Daddy's old medical school friends. Uncle Elmore and Aunt Clara were also in line with us. The small talk among them began to take turn in the direction of "Oh, how wonderful that Buchanan has found such a lovely woman." Kitty proclaimed vehemently. "Don't you dare compare her to Bet! She is NOTHING like her!" Kitty had already seen the handwriting on the wall, but his out-of-town friends I think were like us. We hoped and prayed that this would be a good move for Daddy. It was looking more and more doubtful.

I was glad we had put careful thought into what we wore. We did indeed see many, many people we hadn't seen in a coon's age. I am glad we had listened to Mama when she preached her rules of dress: When in doubt, under dress! No white shoes after Labor Day! Pearls are always appropriate! No black or white at a wedding! Never wear shabby shoes. Always have clean hair! Of course, her list went on and on. I even had gloves and a clean dainty handkerchief in my bag.

She also had rules for what to do when you find yourself in an uncomfortable social situation. One was to smile and find someone to talk to who may be as uncomfortable as you and you'll both feel better. Bessie and I talked a lot that day. When I finally got into the fellowship hall, I found Daddy sitting in a dark corner, on a too small ladder-back chair with his cane, breathing with difficulty. I knew he wanted to be anywhere else. I almost felt sorry for him.

I was barely surprised by this time to see that there was no resemblance of her menu at the reception to what we had originally planned for the rehearsal party. This feast would never have been mistaken for leftovers from anywhere! Unfortunately, we let her buffalo us many more times before it was all over. In her mind, we only did the measly rehearsal party. They did the grand reception. She and her children not only outdid us, they undid us.

After the wedding the possessive, solicitous bride and wheezing groom left for a short trip before they left for the real honeymoon... a romantic lover's cruise. Did I mention that Mama had begged and begged Daddy to take her on a trip? They were constantly being invited places... She always wanted to go and he didn't. She was from the school that believed married women didn't travel alone – or maybe she was too scared to go alone. Whatever the case, she was always disappointed when he wouldn't go. It never stopped her from trying again and again. Along comes The Widow and off he goes! It was sad to think about for Mama. But she did have him when he was younger and more active. She hated it when he got to be so sedentary.

That night after the wedding, and before The Widow officially took possession of Mama's house, we made one last minute decision that we couldn't have known would have been the last time the children truly enjoyed being together in Daddy's home. We decided to let the older grandchildren have a spend-the-night party at the house. Of course, we got caught, but we didn't care. The Widow had forgotten her make-up case and had to come by the house to get it. Daddy called it her "tackle box" with her "lures". I bet she worried that we would mess something up or take something that she might want. Scott and I were the official babysitters that night.

We pulled out rollaway beds, made pallets, romped, popped popcorn, laughed and had a big time! The next day we all ate leftovers together. At the time, we thought our home was safe, especially since we knew that eventually the home would belong to Bessie, as Daddy had always promised. We thought the good family times there would be endless. We had spent virtually all holidays in that home. We had courted there. We had grown up there. New babies had been introduced there. There had been Thanksgivings, Christmases, and Easters, ballgames, picnics and fun. There had also been tears, sickness, and disappointment. We thought this would remain a place of sanctuary for us. Of course nothing stays the same.

CHAPTER 19
"Rise and shine!" Mama

Afto the "honeymoon night," Daddy and The Widow left for the cruise. That seemed a funny choice since their relationship was supposedly platonic, for companionship only. Daddy made a big point of explaining "that" to us. I bet she thought she could fix THAT, too.

Now as he was to be gone on my birthday, he told me "Happy Birthday" before he left. Again, I had no idea that would be the last time he ever acknowledged my birthday. Mama had always been a birthday celebrating type. She would sing up the stairs "Happy Birthday To You" first thing in the morning instead of the usual "Rise and shine." She would cook a nice breakfast, honor your request for supper – mine was usually chicken curry with all the condiments – and of course provide a special gift and a cake. There would be candles and a rousing, if not a little off-key rendition of the "Happy Birthday Song." There would be cards, maybe a party, and the coveted birthday cash, supplied by Daddy. His shopping for gifts, whatever the occasion was limited to going to the bank and getting a gift envelope and giving cash with the face of a president looking through an oval in the envelope. We loved it!

But Mama was more into thoughtful surprises. For Mama, he would go to the jewelry store and buy her some trinket that the jeweler talked him into buying. I'm not sure she always appreciated his gifts. She felt like he was more interested in pleasing the person he was buying from than her but she never let on to him. She enjoyed buying and giving gifts to family and friends. We had the best of all worlds and didn't know it. It was hard to go cold turkey from all the hoopla to zilch.

The second Christmas they were married, after none of the children's, grandchildren's, or even the new great grandchild's birthdays had been acknowledged by even a card, we decided they couldn't remember when they all were and that they were afraid they'd leave someone out. We thought we were being quite thoughtful to give them a calendar with all the birthdays noted. Birthdays still went unrecognized. Just before Daddy died, when he finally began to see the light, he did verbally say "Happy Birthday" to Bessie and Buchanan.

However, The Widow's children's gifts did not diminish during the marriage; in fact, I bet they grew bigger. I know that because she seemed to take great pride in showing us and telling us what she had gotten them. She even gave her children expensive laser eye operations... Never mind that Buchanan and I were as nearsighted as bats and were great candidates for the surgery. Daddy did not know what she was doing for them. When she talked about how they didn't overdo and give extravagant gifts he believed her! Besides, it wasn't long before she had him believing we were ungrateful, money-grubbing children who had been spoiled and already had all we deserved. I faulted him for believing this. If the truth is to be admitted, we did have all the material things we needed. It wasn't the things that upset us as much as the loss of our Father and his love and respect. Daddy slowly became a stranger. He fell into The Widow's web. She never failed to point out how good her children were to him. How they brought him Godiva Chocolates, not just the cheap Russell Stover outlet bags like Grand Mama Bethea used to keep that we brought.

Grand Mama would go to the seconds store in Marion, get a box or bag of chocolates and keep them in the vegetable drawer in her refrigerator. She would indulge herself one after supper each evening. She kept in her other vegetable drawer six-ounce bottled coca-colas. We loved to be allowed an occasional treat from her refrigerator when we were visiting. Once when Grand Mama went with us for an outing we got locked out. Grand Mama's security system consisted of a huge climbing pyracantha bush growing around her bedroom windows. Her bedroom was a later addition. When his emphysema incapacitated Pop, she had a small bedroom built on half of the porch adjacent their bedroom. There was a window separating the doors. She could nurse him and sleep. After Pop died she continued to sleep in the little pink bedroom with the dotty chenille bedspread and white ruffled organdy tie back curtains. The only thing masculine about that room was the other part of her security system, a fully loaded revolver she kept in her beside table. They say she was a sharpshooter. She kept her bedroom door locked when children visited. Anna Bet says she remembers how they were never allowed to even go near that room.

Back to the lockout! BJ who was three at the time was with us on this particular outing. There was an opening in the porch window over the thorny bush. I maneuvered BJ through the window, incurring scratches galore on my arms. We promised him a treat from the refrigerator if he would go in and open the door for us. Well, went in, he did, but instead of opening the door for us, he went straight to the old Frigidaire, got out his Co-cola, opened it himself on the bottle opener Grand Mama had screwed into her kitchen cabinet casing; and sat down on her spotless linoleum floor. We frantically banged and yelled, trying to get him to let us in. He ignored us. When he had sufficiently quenched his thirst, he let us in. If I'd been a drinking woman I would have wanted something harder than a Co-cola right then.

CHAPTER 20
"Pretty is as pretty does." Mama

In addition to their so-called generosity, The Widow never failed to point out how pretty her girls were, and how elegantly dressed. Now I know I'm no beauty, never have been… but Bessie and JoNelle both were. Why, JoNelle was Miss Kingston! All of our girls are absolutely beautiful…every one of them. Even I could clean up when need be. But Daddy soon was convinced that her side was the pretty side! I'd say they were the prissy side.

She never failed to point out how artistically talented her grandchildren were. One of them was such a budding artist that they gave her our grandmother's leather paint case and easel. Never mind that several of his own grandchildren, BJ, Anna Bet, Mary Ann, and Sarah Beth had all won art awards! Daddy was soon convinced that the others were the artistic side… and said so.

She never failed to point out how musically talented she was. Not long after they were married, she replaced her small "punch-the-bass-key-for-a-rhythm-organ" for a fancier model. Daddy was convinced she was a concert pianist. After Lori, Leslie, Mary Ann and Anna Belle played recital pieces on the piano for them; she sort of quieted down on that issue. She could play simple hymns for the Sunday school class. That added to her nobility, but not to her talent.

CHAPTER 21
"Work first, play later." Mama

*W*e never were encouraged to be prissy. Mama was feminine, beautiful, but not prissy. She was proud that she didn't "waste" her time and money in the weekly ritual of the beauty parlor, where many of her friends, went to have their hair dyed, permed, and stiffened so that it would not move until the next week when the cycle was repeated. We called it having hair "fixed." She didn't have to. Mama's naturally curly, prematurely gray hair was always beautiful. She claimed to have trouble finding someone to cut it properly. She would enlist my college roommate, a sharp mathematician and self-made beautician, to cut her hair looking nice. Mama didn't have to be prissy to keep her hair. She could let it blow in the wind, get wet, and just run her fingers through it to "fix" it. Before car air conditioners became a standard feature, we had to endure many a sweltering ride so as not to "mess-up" somebody's hair do. Because of this prissiness, many women and young girls missed out on the joy of a ride in an open boat, a walk in the rain, a quick swim in the ocean or a water-skiing outing on the Waccamaw River. Not Mama! She loved these things and taught us to love them too.

The only make up she ever wore was lipstick and loose powder. She loved lavender soap, Jergen's lotion and talcum powder. When she was really dressed up she put on her White Shoulders perfume. I remember her going out to the Riverside Club New Year's Eve Party in her rhinestone jewelry, swishy taffeta black dress and perfume. I thought she looked like a movie star. She loved to dance, laugh, and *flirt. She smoked her Lucky Strikes unfiltered cigarettes with the flair of the glamorous. Sadly, her death from the lung cancer was anything but glamorous.*

We grew up as beach bums, not priss pots, as The Widow once called Bessie. Mama and the children would load up the old station wagon with our toys, books, and food packed in cardboard boxes, our old English setter, Mark, the parakeet, Peatie, and head for the beach. We were one of the few two-car families in town at the time. Mama used to say that every time she thought they had a little change in their pockets, Daddy would buy a new car. Then she'd get his old one. She would complain about the new hand-me-down, always saying she liked the old one better. She was not all about cars. One of Daddy's old medical buddies came to visit once and he was driving a big black Mercedes-Benz. Mama asked, "Are they having hard times, having to drive that old car?"

We wouldn't come home until time for school to start, unless a hurricane came. Then we'd load the station wagon, usually with Kitty and Cooper along too, and head back to Kingston to ride out the storm. During the summers, Kitty and Cooper just molded into our family. We had no TV at the beach and of course there was no Doppler radar or very accurate weather predictions. I remember the flag pole at Withers Swash with the red flag squares with the black squares in the center, snapping in the wind, warning of the approaching storm as we stopped to pick-up Kitty and Cooper. We thought it was all very exciting.

One time they forgot something and we had to go back to the old house they called The Barnacle. Ordinarily, they would have never locked the house, but this particular time they did. They only way to get into the house was through a very small open window in the kitchen. Kitty got stuck trying to get through the tiny window. What a sight! I remember everyone laughing until our sides nearly split, including Kitty.

When Hurricane Hazel backtracked and devastated Myrtle Beach in the fall of 1954, Mama and Daddy were on one of their rare trips to High Hampton in the mountains for a medical convention. They could get no news except that the hurricane had hit and they were frantic. We happily rode out the storm at Sam's office, a safe concrete structure, with all the dogs. We thought it was fun to have the electricity go out and to watch from the windows as the trees cracked off or toppled over, bringing up the roots as they toppled. I know now that we were very fortunate. Our beach house was not even damaged. Then a hurricane was just an exciting adventure. I know I shouldn't, but I still find hurricane weather exciting.

In those days, Myrtle Beach was a family beach, and we lived in an enclave of families primarily from Kingston. The daddies all commuted to town to work. The Mamas and children whiled away the summer days in the easy, relaxed atmosphere of the beach.

One time there was a huge forest fire between Kingston and Myrtle Beach. Daddy couldn't get to the beach and Rosa couldn't go home. For some unremembered reason, Buchanan wanted to go to Kingston and said that he would just walk! Rosa was too stout to run very fast and I had to go catch him, pick him up and bring him back, kicking and screaming. It was scary enough with the black ashes raining down and the smoke bellowing up. I was worried and felt somehow I must protect us. After the fire was put out, someone put up those big, Smokey the Bear signs saying, "Only YOU can prevent forest fires." I wondered what I should have done.

Our days at the beach followed a pattern, almost as regular as the tides. We would rise early, dress in our morning bathing suits, eat breakfast, do our chores and head for the beach. We became very efficient dishwashers, bed-makers and sweepers, knowing we could not go on the beach until the work was done. We'd stay out all morning. We were not allowed out past the breakers unless the water was very calm and the tide was rising. Mama constantly warned of the rip tides and undertow and we had to stay exactly in front of where she and the other ladies sat and talked on the beach. Sometimes the mothers would mortify us by doing their exercise routines on the beach. We reserved our more adventurous, deeper swimming until late afternoon when Daddy came home and took us out. In late summer we had to watch for the stinging jellyfish. Daddy taught us to body surf and Mama taught us to make drip castles.

We all became excellent swimmers. Bessie had to overcome a real fear of water that came about when she was a baby. A hysterical man came to our beach house banging on the door and screaming for the doctor. His daughter had drowned and they had been unable to revive her. Bessie was terrified. Mama had to finally become a "swimming-team Mama" so that Bessie could finally overcome her fear, more easily done in a pool setting than in the ocean. Fortunately, today Bessie loves swimming in the ocean.

After spending the morning on the beach, we'd come up for lunch, usually tomato sandwiches, cucumbers, either cantaloupe or peaches, and milk. Tomato sandwiches were the staple of our diet. The soft white bread would stick to the roofs of our mouths and the juicy seeds would sometimes dribble down our chins.

Belle loves fresh, homegrown tomatoes, too. Her first taste of fresh tomatoes came before she was even one. Daddy had a vegetable garden. One he was quite proud of, I might add. He made "bras" for his cantaloupes out of plastic netting that onions come in from the grocery store, so that they would not break off the vine prematurely. Once when he was going out of town he asked me to pick his garden for him. I had Belle in her stroller, trudging through the sandy rows. I stopped to wrestle with some prickly okra. When I turned my attention to Belle, she had helped herself to a red, vine-ripe tomato. She bit into it like it was an apple. Thank heaven there was no pesticide on Daddy's tomatoes. She, too, had tomato juice dribbling down her chin.

One of my friends from Pendleton says she remembers sitting on the back porch with her mother, who was slicing a tomato and putting it on a fresh homemade biscuit. They were talking about heaven, when her Mama said, "You know, heaven will be a land of milk and honey. Linda said to her mama, "I like milk but do you think God might let us have tomato sandwiches instead of honey?" That kind of sums up how I feel.

After lunch we had to take a "Polio nap". Now when I look back on the polio nap, I wonder if that wasn't just an excuse to keep us quiet for a while to give Mama and Kitty some peace until we could go back out on the beach. Whatever the case, we each had to go to a separate room for a two-hour "nap". Most often I would stretch out on the cotton bedspread play possum when Mama looked in, and then sneak-read the hours away.

They didn't just use polio for nap excuse either. They told us that it was not safe to be in large crowds. We could seldom go the movies or the pavilion. We went only once in the early spring and had a very limited budget. Mama thought this part of the beach was tacky and tawdry and we were not allowed to indulge in the souvenir shops or the more seedy side of beach life, at least until we were teenagers and escaped parental watchfulness. To me the beach had and still has a split personality.

When we went to the movies it was mostly to the drive-in theater. We would pile up the station wagon, flatten the back seat, cover it with blankets and pillows and watch the movie. We would attach-the tinny-sounding speaker to the car window, watch the mosquito repellant ads and the ads for the concessions, which we never bought, the previews, the cartoons and finally the movie. Bessie would always fall asleep. I guess Mama took us to the movies when Daddy was "on-call" and stayed in Kingston. She and Kitty would sort of sit sideways in the front seat, as we had backed into the parking spot. We usually had to try several speakers until we found one that worked.

Mama also didn't trust food handlers who cooked corn-dogs, cotton candy, or even the boiled peanuts. She said they handled money and didn't wash their hands afterwards. She was all about proper food handling; maybe the polio thing was a part of this. Perhaps it was her training as a nutritionist and her work in the hospital before she met Daddy. She hated dishrags, sponges and dirty washcloths. When paper towels became popular, she embraced them with a passion!

The polio scare was probably real. I remember when the Salk vaccine came out and Daddy went to the school where children lined up for the inoculations. I remember the pictures of iron lungs in "Life Magazine" and going to college with girls whose legs were wasted by the disease. Whatever the truth was, we took polio naps.

After the nap, we went back down on the beach, or to the camp we had in the scrub oak and pinewoods next to the house. We had a small hammock back there and Buchanan was forever building "traps" for us and trying to lead us into them. In the afternoon we could not swim until Daddy got home. By then the sea breeze had usually picked up, the sea was rough with whitecaps and the undertow was strong.

If it were low tide, we might go shelling especially around Hurl rocks. My system was to pick up a broken shell until I found a whole one like it, and then discard the broken one. We found and collected a variety of sizes, shapes, and colors indigenous to the area. We would string them together for jewelry, mount them for pictures, decorate with them, use them for paperweights and doorstops, and Mama and her friends would use them for ashtrays. I still have some that I keep in one of my Charleston baskets.

Sometimes, rather than go back down on the beach, we'd sit on the porch, rock, and play cards. We would spend the summer trying to find a license plate from each state. It became a lot harder when Alaska and Hawaii became states. We loved to watch for dolphins, to watch the seagulls hunt, and to follow the dark spots in the ocean created by schools of fish as they moved up the beach.

If it rained, we played cards, Clue and Monopoly, put together puzzles, and produced and performed plays for the adults. The primary living area of the beach house was on the upper level. The lower level was later closed in and a concrete floor, a bathroom, and bedrooms were added. The children had the run of this part of the house. This is where we spent rainy days. We could spend the whole afternoon rehearsing and making costumes for an evening performance. Even so it turned out to be mostly ad-lib and slapstick with a lot of fake-fighting violence.

When we were growing up, discipline was not looked upon as child abuse if parents used the belt or a switch. I only remember two physical punishments, and both of them were at the beach. Mama mostly just lectured on and on. I often wished she would just spank us and get it over with. Bessie's best friend Katie, Sam and Verda Lee's daughter, recalled how Mama would start her long-winded discussions and explanations. She said Bessie would just ease up the stairs and leave her there to have to politely hear her out.

Daddy would occasionally resort to the belt. If we were getting out of hand, all he had to do was fiddle with his belt buckle and we'd straighten up and fly right. He used it _very_ rarely. Once though, at the beach when we had company I must have thought I had him over a barrel. We were all sitting around the old pine picnic table that served as the dining table. At the beach house, everything was simple and sturdy. Mama left her fineries at home and brought to the beach the things that were shabby but were too good to throw away. So, as we sat around the old table eating breakfast, I must have been showing-off, for when Daddy told me to settle down and eat my breakfast, the thirteen year old me told him I didn't like the way the eggs were cooked and I wasn't going to do it. I don't remember my feet touching the floor as he grabbed my elbow and herded me off to the bedroom. He let me know I was not too old for a spanking. He hurt our feelings more than anything, and then we'd start to cry. I remember him saying, "Stop crying or I'll give you something to cry about!" I still don't understand that expression.

One of our next-door neighbors had a scream and slap discipline style. She would scream and scream and then "Pow"! You would hear a sharp slap and one of her children usually would be crying. When I was older I learned that the Daddy too, was pretty heavy handed; he sure was more likeable than the Mama though. She scared me.

One time, again when I was at that sassy, talkback stage, Mama slapped my face. We were both shocked. Mama went upstairs and cried all afternoon. I was bewildered, especially when she apologized. I guess her patience had just reached its limit that day. After raising daughters myself, - I know just how she felt. I never slapped them, though.

With the exceptions of our dolls, Terri Lee and Jerri Lee, Buchanan got punished the most. He seemed to find more ways to get in trouble. Bessie would tell on him for some misdemeanor, and then cry when he got punished.

We played dolls by the hours at the beach. We would take the dolls on long trips in the parked station wagon. They stayed in their bathing suits most of the day, and of course put on their pajamas every night. When Harriette and I decided it was time to lose Bessie we'd let her baby-sit. If our dolls misbehaved, we'd beat the tar out of them. Poor dolls. Harriette and I had Terri Lee and Jerri Lee dolls, as well as the baby Linda Lee. We had innumerable outfits for them. I'm ashamed to tell you how old we were before we quit playing dolls. I still have Terri and Jerri, as well as most of their clothes.

When Daddy got home in later afternoon, we'd swim in the rough ocean, then come back and shower. In the outdoor shower if we forgot our clothes, we'd just scamper up the back stairs wrapped in a towel or not, depending on who was there. Then we'd have supper. Rosalee would ride the bus to the beach each morning, fix supper and do light housekeeping, and ride back to Kingston on the bus.

After supper we may churn ice cream, cut a watermelon, or on rare occasions stop the Hubba-Hubba man for a treat. The Hubba-

Hubba man drove the ice-cream truck down the boulevard with his tinkley music attracting youngster like the Pied Piper. We saved our allowances for the treats he offered. I liked the vanilla ice cream that was dipped in a chocolate coating with toffee chips in the chocolate. All food tastes better at the beach, after you have been swimming most of the day.

After dark, we would sit a while on the porch, and watch the fireflies or the moon over the ocean. Lots of evenings there would be a thunderstorm to watch. Sometimes there was only sheet lightning and gentle thunder. At other times the lightning was sharp and the thunder shook the house. Very rarely, there would be no breeze at all and the biting sand gnats came through the screens. Usually when we would go off to bed, the sea-breeze would blow the curtains straight out and you could hear the high pitched whine of the wind whistling through the screens, the quiet crash of ocean waves and the cicadas and frogs singing us to sleep. Life was good!

I guess Mama had it made in many ways. No wonder when Daddy decided to sell the beach house when we were older, Mama had a fit. Daddy was like that. He would make decisions without getting her input. That time he went too far. I don't think she ever forgave him.

When I grew older, I knew more about prissy girls at the beach, but we were forever beach bums. The Widow was not. She was prissy.

CHAPTER 22
"The way to a man's heart is through his stomach."
Mama

One thing The Widow could never do better than us is cook. We came from a long line of good cooks. *Mama of course, was noted for her cooking, especially to be able to go to the cabinet, pull out a bit of this and that, grab something from a can and produce a tasty meal for one or twenty. Daddy came home for lunch every day, and she always had it waiting for him. Then he would retreat to his room, undress and take a nap before returning to work. It was definite QUIET HOUR at our house during Daddy's naptime.*

Grand Mama too was a great cook as was Kaye. We were used to fine dinners. JoNelle and her mama are both great cooks and Bessie and I don't do too badly. In contrast Daddy and The Widow went out to lunch daily. He ate cereal for breakfast, went out to lunch, and drank for supper. Mama taught us how to entertain with ease.

Several years into their marriage, Daddy had a heart attack and was taken to Providence in Columbia by helicopter where he had by-pass surgery. Bessie and Buchanan and Kaye and The Widow and I all sat in the waiting room... Uncle Elmore and Aunt Clara came and Mama's stepsister, and some of The Widow's children, too. Bessie and I stayed in the same hotel in Columbia. We were in and out of the hospital while Daddy was there. Daddy was hooked up to all those wires and tubes and of course little visiting was allowed or appropriate. You would have thought The Widow had never been around anybody sick before. She acted all hysterical and gloom and doom. Mama had the same surgery, years ago when it was still experimental. The doctors assured us that Daddy was doing well. In fact, he was sent home in just a few days. Well, I guess we didn't weep and wail enough to suit The Widow. She convinced herself that she, and only she, cared about Daddy. You know how people are in La-La land right after surgery? Daddy did not even remember that we were there. The Widow did not correct his mistaken idea. He thought that she and her children were the only ones who came. I guess it suited her purpose to let him think that. Never mind that Bessie and Lou were the ones she called and who saw to him in every emergency. He was convinced not only that we did not care about him, but also that he had to have someone, namely her, around to care for him. The web wrapped tighter.

After the surgery, The Widow seemed to make little, if any effort, to provide proper meals for Daddy. Of course, it could be argued that he was a grown man, and could have taken responsibility for his own recovery, I suppose. He just came from an era when men didn't usually expect to do so. I remember Hub saying that her attitude of neglect was criminal. He wondered if Daddy suffered from malnutrition.

I could count on my hands the meals we shared at Daddy's after they married. One Thanksgiving, though we did eat there. I again came pretty close to feeling sorry for her. The meal was awful. The turkey was dry, the gravy was watery and the dressing was so salty it couldn't be swallowed. Scott and the children were eating on the patio. I understand there was a great deal of unmannerly spitting food into the boxwoods. She even served baked beans. They certainly did seem out of place in the silver-serving dish, but they tasted pretty good. It was like she could not decide whether we were having a bar-be-que or a formal dinner. The only other big meal I remember was a birthday party for Daddy. Her children brought most of that food. Thankfully, Jannie did cook for Daddy some. In defense of The Widow she could make a good cake! I guess "Let them eat cake!" was her philosophy.

Very shortly after Daddy's by-pass there was some sort of gathering of The Widow's family in Rock Hill. That week there was one of those stretches of weather we call dog days. The daytime temperatures hovered near 100 and evenings were in the 80's. There were no cooling breezes unless there were late afternoon storms, and even those just upped the already breath-taking, glasses fogging humidity. Heat advisories abounded. We were urged to check on the elderly, particularly those with breathing problems. (Hello! Daddy!) All along the highways were cars that had died of heat exhaustion with those little red flags on them. You could see heat waves rising in ripples along the horizon of the highway. The heat was miserable and dangerous.

Bessie had the gall to suggest that maybe they postpone the trip until the weather broke. The Widow was livid! This is when in her fury, she called Bessie a "priss-pot". Daddy just sat there and allowed The Widow to call Bessie names. What happened to the strong father who had protected us and kept us safe? The strong man in the soft suit who smelled of Sir Walter Raleigh and Old Spice? We couldn't even express concerns? Dr. Palmer, our neighbor who let Daddy know in no uncertain terms that he should not go, finally resolved the issue. He hadn't even had his first check-up since the by-pass. The Widow was still livid, and we all knew it.

Not long after that she told Buchanan to "go to

Hell, "in front of the younger Buchanan. It seems Buchanan came upon Daddy and The Widow in a heated discussion. Buchanan now experienced the same feeling of rejection that Bessie had. Daddy at first chose to believe The Widow. He said she wouldn't have said such a thing to Buchanan. Only when JoNelle let him know that Buchanan R. was there did he believe it.

Another sore spot for all of us, but particularly Buchanan, was Daddy's Citadel ring. Academics were the easy part of getting through the Citadel. Plebes had to go through severe hazing. It was mighty rough but in Daddy's day no one dared complain. Many, many, just quit. To make it through was quite an ordeal. The Citadel ring was a symbol of completing this struggle. Daddy wore it with pride. Occasionally, he would bonk us on the head with it to quiet us down. To us, it was an extension of his hand; he always wore it.

Buchanan, too, graduated from the Citadel. In fact, Daddy presented him his diploma. Imagine our chagrin when shortly after Daddy died, she showed up in Sunday school wearing it. It had been remade into a necklace. Me Maw was the first of us to know. She hated to tell JoNelle because she knew how upset Buchanan would be. She was right. He was, but not surprised. Buchanan should have had that ring, too.

We knew exactly where we stood. The Widow was in the driver's seat, literally. She drove Daddy almost everywhere and had full control. He was afraid he'd be alone. He was afraid to cross her. The changes in our relationship with Daddy were subtle but tough. We still all got together at Christmas, and at other times during the year, but it wasn't fun with The Widow. She never let him out of her sight, it felt like.

CHAPTER 23

"It's just as easy to love a rich man as it is to love a poor man." Mama's Mama

The physical changes continued in Daddy's house. By now we were resigned to these changes, and truthfully, the yard really began to look more cared for, if not a bit overdone.

The white-wall, though, thoroughly desecrated Daddy's den. The focal point of the den was a wide, spacious fireplace. Surrounding the fireplace was a hearth built from old brick salvaged from a warehouse from Mama's beloved Charleston. In fact the exterior of the house was also built of old Charleston brick. The hearth was the very best of the brick, hand-picked by Mama. The fireplace, along with the pickled-pine paneling, wide ceiling beams and old pine mantle helped create a room that was warm, welcoming and cozy. Daddy used to love to build a roaring fire. He built coal fires for a while, but then switched to wood. I can remember Mama's white head shining through the broad windows as she sat on the sofa late at night waiting on us as teenagers to come in. If we sat in the driveway too long, she would blink the proverbial lights at us.

The Widow covered up the fireplace with a glass screen that made it smaller and put in gas logs. I almost could see the practicality of that, although I love a real fire. She put plywood over the area above the mantle and covered it with blue wallpaper; she painted beneath the mantle and the hearth white. We could hardly believe it! Fortunately Bessie and JoNelle warned me before I came for a visit. Even being forewarned, I was still shocked to see it. The Widow asked me what I thought of it. The only nice thing I could think of to say was, "It will take some getting used to". We still did not want to be rude and express our true reactions in front of Daddy.

As the years went on Daddy became more and more depressed and reclusive. His days followed a dreary predictability that I'm sure was not easy for The Widow. He would go to the drugstore, the bank, and return home to work crossword puzzles in his bed. They would go to lunch at Donzelle's. Then he would nap, they would go for a little ride, and he would be home by 5PM; and fix his first bullbat. The only variation was where they went for a ride. He went to bed by dark every night. He was ornery and stubborn and easily irritated. I understand that he was not very pleasant to live with. He would often get up in the night to fix a snack. Every now and then he'd fall and The Widow would call Bessie to come help him back to bed. At first she had tried calling EMT to help, but I think he thoroughly embarrassed her with his choice of words directed toward them. If he seemed hurt after that, Dr. Palmer would come from next door to check on him. I know that when The Widow married him, she had an inkling of what he was really like, but like most of us, I think she thought she could change him, make him happy. When the gala charity evenings, trips abroad, and the summers in Maine did not materialize I am sure she had to be disappointed.

I think he knew how disappointed she was and tried to appease her. I think that may be why he decided to change his will and give her the house and its belongings instead of lifetime rights, and to also give her a considerable cash settlement, despite the pre-nuptial agreement, which The

Widow hated. I suspect that he agreed to things after he was in his cups and then had too much pride to admit he couldn't remember. Whatever the case, I know he felt like his money was his chief asset and that folks were often nice to him because they thought he had some. He often said so. I remember him telling his cousin Billy that the reason he hadn't remarried was that his bank account wasn't big enough.

Unfortunately, Bessie heard of news about the house from Mrs. Palmer, Daddy's next-door neighbor, in the aisle of Winn Dixie. Bernice asked The Widow who would get the house when she died, and she replied, "My children of course." By now Bessie was deeply hurt, but not crushed. We had come to anticipate this sort of thing. When Daddy finally got around to telling us, it was old news.

CHAPTER 24
"Don't glide through that stop sign!" Daddy

Eventually, all this became too much for The Widow. She needed to get away. Now that she needed our help, she became much more cordial. She called me in Greenwood to ask if I'd come stay with Daddy while she went on a cruise. It was to be in June and school would be out and I would have just retired (though not permanently). Belle was going to be in Governor's School in Charleston. The timing was perfect. I called Bessie, and she agreed with trepidation to help me. We were very nervous. We certainly didn't want something to happen, especially while The Widow was gone, so that she could blame us. Yet we really looked forward to spending time at our old home with Daddy.

By now Daddy had become very feeble physically. He had to take oxygen everywhere he went and could hardly walk. He might use a cane from time to time but absolutely refused to seriously try a walker. The Widow said he refused to eat.

We began our week together. The first night we were there, Bessie and I could hardly sleep. We kept checking on Daddy like he was a newborn to see if he were breathing. We tried to follow Daddy's daily schedule. We found he ate a plenty, when we gave him what he liked. He was especially fond of pineapple milkshakes, bananas, peanut butter sandwiches, cashews, maple nut goodies and ethnic foods like egg fu young, lasagna, and curries.

The afternoon rides were fun and interesting, except that Daddy was an outspoken back-seat driver. He watched the speedometer like a hawk and treated us like we were teenagers just learning to drive. He warned us about every likely and unlikely danger he could anticipate. Bessie and I would argue like children over whose turn it was to drive. Neither of use wanted the job. I'll bet he did The Widow the same way.

One particular day we went to Marion on our outing. We rode around as he revisited and pointed out to us his old school, his Grandparents' home, his home, the old tobacco farm, his Daddy's old office, the spot on the Pee Dee River where he learned to swim and, finally the graves of many relatives, including his parents. He shared many memories with obvious relish. Bessie and I were really enjoying the comradeship. About the time we were at the cemetery, we must have over-expressed our enthusiasm. He said dryly, "Oh, joy! Now I guess we need to go to the mortuary!"

On the way home that day, he decided he needed to stop at the liquor store to restock. We told him we'd drive him but we weren't going in to buy it for him. We pulled into a red-dot store in Marion and he told us we couldn't stop at that particular undesirable location. He directed that we stop in Aynor. We stopped, opened the door for him and watched him teeter toward the liquor store. We had second thoughts about letting him try to go alone so I got out and followed behind him, I guess thinking I might break his fall if he toppled over. By now he was pretty hot with Bessie and me. He went in, made his purchase, and started shakily but resolutely back to the car. He actually moved with more vigor than I had seen in quite a while. Bessie and I decided later that if we could have put his bottle at the end of a walking course, he might have gotten more exercise. Anyway, the proprietor of the liquor store, one of those feisty, bossy ladies came out of the store and flat told Bessie and me off. She put her finger in our faces and let us know in no uncertain terms that we should have come in and made his purchase for him. Who knows? I never asked The Widow if she ever bought liquor for him. I'll bet she didn't. I know that Buchanan was dispatched to the store from time to time. I think Daddy also had a delivery system set up with one of the local red-dot store owners. Whoever he traded with had a good customer.

One night though, when The Widow called from the cruise, I heard him begging her to come home and that he promised he would do better if she wouldn't leave him. I don't know exactly what he meant. I was appalled at how dependent and afraid he had become. With the exception of the liquor store incident, we really had a wonderful week.

Daddy enjoyed himself, and the house was once again full of friends and family; Buchanan came every night. Lots of Daddy's old friends came by while The Widow was gone. Some of them didn't feel welcome when she was at home. This was the last time we were ever a part of Daddy's active life.

CHAPTER 25
"People are more important than things."
Mama

When The Widow returned, things went back to the way they were between us. His depression deepened and he became feebler, physically. His health deteriorated to the point that he was hospitalized and his mental sharpness began to wane. The Widow decided that she could no longer handle things and decided to move him to an assisted living facility. Didn't work. He fussed, and cussed and regressed to the point that she realized she best get him back home. He was even more difficult and demanding at the nursing home. We suggested that he go home, but that she get round-the-clock help. Certainly Daddy could afford it. If he couldn't have we would have seen to it that he had help or we would have been there. She agreed to get help at night. I really don't think she wanted to have extra folks around all the time. I know she didn't want us. She was not very accommodating to the help either. There was a comfortable chair in the room, perfect for a sitter. She insisted on moving it out. Said the chair would get soiled from folks resting their heads on the chair and that they might fall asleep. That was a typical response for her. Things are more important than people. The exact opposite of Mama's philosophy. We were fortunate that the nurse and her daughter, Tonya, stayed with Daddy and knew him from way back when, and tolerated the situation. In fact, they were wonderful to him. When I had to leave to go back to Greenwood, I felt more secure having them there.

Daddy's final months were strange. Dr. Dietrich said that physically there was no reason Daddy should be going down so quickly. It's like something just snapped and he gave up. Once when he was in the hospital, Dr. Dietrich furiously asked, "Who has told him he is dying?" Well, The Widow didn't tell him to his face, but when anyone called or came by, she went into a long litany about how badly he was doing. She talked about him like he was invisible. He wasn't as sharp as he used to be, but he was not senile, either.

In fact, if anything he seemed more aware that he had let himself be taken advantage of. On one occasion, he called The Widow "money grubbing", in front of the nurse. The nurse was deeply concerned about him. She told us that he perked up considerably when we came by, that he acted like a different person. She kept hoping he would snap out of his blues. But Daddy was a stubborn man. He'd rather go to his grave than admit a mistake. Especially such a big mistake as marrying a casserole widow!

Soon Daddy was practically bed-ridden. He sometimes imagined he was still practicing medicine and worried about his patients. Other times he was clear minded. The Widow had agreed finally to have full-time help, including a trained orderly, Laverne, from the hospital who helped Daddy bathe. Daddy's dignity would not allow such help from the female nurses. Buchanan had been helping him, as well.

Buchanan had power-of-attorney and handled the logistics of moving money from accounts as needed. Before Daddy came home from the hospital The Widow tried to go to the bank and get into Daddy's safe deposit box. She was incensed when the bank would not let her. I think she promptly moved her personal account to another bank. At least she said she was going to.

I think it galled her that Daddy had continued to trust Buchanan instead of her to handle his personal finances. In what I think was a ploy to change this, The Widow told the nurse, in front of Daddy, that she must let them go, for there was not enough money to pay for help. Fortunately, instead of believing The Widow, she knew to call Buchanan. He immediately straightened that out.

What was so unfortunate for Daddy about this situation was that we all knew that in matters affecting finances, Daddy was scrupulously honest. He could not abide dishonestly. The surest way to a spanking from Daddy was to let him catch you in a lie. Bessie and I didn't try it much, but when he was a child Buchanan could look him in the eye and tell a bald-faced lie. When he got caught, he figured it was worth the gamble, since he often did not get caught. I have little gambling spirit.

Not long ago I learned of an incident in Daddy's childhood, which may have played a factor in his great aversion to dishonesty. Prior to the crash of '29 and the resulting run on the banks, Pop was an employee of a local bank, as well as a tobacco farmer. As near as I can find out, from Annie Huggins whose father-in-law was also involved, Pop and Mr. Huggins took the fall when the bank failed for apparently approving unsecured loans, or something of that sort. Whatever the case, Pop and Mr. Huggins had to serve a short time in the gentleman's jail to atone for the bank's failure. I understand they were in very good company and that they took the punishment for others above them. In any case, Pop's reputation as a business man remained untarnished and he returned to later build up a reputable insurance company that catered to the needs of the local farmers – hail insurance and stuff like that. Pop's small business was sold after his death to Daddy's cousin who still runs it today.

Because of Grand Mama's stern Baptist upbringing, his strong sense of right and wrong, and the nature of small towns, Daddy was embarrassed and ashamed. He was only a boy at the time and could not have understood. He did not want to do or want us to do anything that could be construed as shady. He prided himself on his integrity, financial and otherwise.

Naturally, when he was told he could not pay his bills, he was distraught. He struggled to get up and tried to dress so that he could go "take care of this matter". Fortunately, Buchanan got there, soothed his worries and convinced him that his financial affairs were in order.

The Widow had another hissy fit when the bank sent the statements to Buchanan instead of to her. Oh, well. We all came by to visit the next weekend. She sat there primly in the den and claimed, "Your Daddy's care is so expensive. I am concerned that it will take all of your inheritances to take care of him."

Hah! Have you ever head anything so absurd? First of all, most of what we were to inherit had already been given to us when Mama died, thanks to Buchanan's accounting foresight. In fact, the sale of some property at Patriot's Point in Charleston insured a secure retirement for me. Not lavish, but with my schoolteacher pension, secure. Most of what we stood left to inherit, she already had. We knew that she had the house, and all its major repairs and improvements done during their nine-year marriage. She had most of the furnishings and household effects that belonged to our parents. She had what we thought to be a considerable cash settlement. And she had the nerve to try to skimp on Daddy's care? Skimp on it with Daddy's own resources, saved for just such purposes?

CHAPTER 26
"...the resurrection of the body."

Bessie and I had stayed with Daddy in June. By early November I got the dreaded call. "You need to come home, NOW". I started for Kingston; Bessie kept calling me on the cell phone to give me updates. I finally got to the hospital and went straight to Daddy's room. The Widow was not there. She had left to go supervise planting pansies in the yard. She returned after a while. I always wondered why the pansies couldn't wait. I guess one has to keep up appearances.

Bessie was in Hell-Hole Swamp on a field trip with her school children when they called her to come. What a time she had getting someone to watch 25 rambunctious fifth graders. As she said, "Thank heaven for good friends"!

He was not conscious when we got there. He was hooked up to the heart monitor that indicated his weakening condition. He had socks on over his very cold feet. His breathing was labored. We knew he was about to leave us. We talked to him as if he could hear us, and from time to time there was a slight response – a squeezing of our hand or a flicker of his eyes. Bessie, Buchanan and I sat on one side of Daddy's bed, near the foot, and The Widow and some of her kinfolk, many I didn't even know, crowded on the other side. We sat talking quietly, listening to the sounds of the monitor. Waiting. Watching. At one point someone removed it. I remember how kind and thoughtful all the medical staff were.

A short time later, The Widow suggested, "Let's all join hands and recite the Apostle's Creed, as Buchanan and I did every night before we went to bed." That was the biggest prevarication I ever heard. I was stunned. Daddy had his type of faith, but reciting the Apostle's Creed before bedtime was definitely not his style. The Lord's Prayer, maybe, but not the Apostles Creed! How she could make up such rubbish at his deathbed was more than I could take.

I got up and walked out of the room, in tears. Right behind me followed Bessie, then Buchanan. We stood huddled together, not knowing exactly what to do. Shortly, along came Tonya. She asked us "What's the matter"? She knew something was wrong. We told her the problem and also told her that we were very uncomfortable with all the strangers standing around watching us watch our Daddy die. When we went back to Daddy's room, Tonya had cleared it out.

It was a long, tough afternoon. Daddy became very restless. Buchanan talked to him and soothed him. The Widow told him to "Go to sleep. I'll see you in the morning". I thought, "What?!!" Finally, Daddy took his last breath and gave up the ghost. We said our final good-byes. We were exhausted. We got up to go. The Widow wanted to stay until they took his body to the funeral home, but we had to get away! We were foolish enough to think that we could better deal with The Widow now that we didn't have to worry so about upsetting Daddy.

CHAPTER 27
"...and exchange it one day for a crown."

W e still had to face the funeral and all the arrangements. To be sure, I only remember bits and pieces of the next few days. We stood by while she made most of the arrangements. She picked the casket, the day, time and location of the services. We wanted a closed casket at the visitation. It was open. Daddy had this thing about young children at funerals. He said he had to deal with the irrational fears developed by many children who were told to kiss their dead relatives good-by. When Pop died, I was in the fifth grade. Certainly I should have been old enough to go, but he thought better. We kept Timmy, Daddy's only great-grandchild, home from the funeral and visitation. All the toddlers in her family came to both, uncomfortably over-dressed and whiney.

After the visitation, we asked to be let back in the funeral parlor so that we could read the cards on the flowers. We wanted to be able to thank our personal friends. We had no other way of knowing who sent what. The Widow rewrote the simple obituary we submitted and printed a longer, pompous sounding one. Fortunately we all agreed on the music, including Daddy's shower hymns, "The Old Rugged Cross" and "The Church in the Valley by the Wildwood".

Later, after Daddy had been dead and buried a while, The Widow had Daddy's grave re-dug and centered to suit her in the plot. We had buried him off-center, close to Mama, leaving space in the plot in case someone else needed to use it.

The flowers for the coffin were the biggest point of contention. She wanted the Oopsy-Daisey to do them and we wanted Harry at the Magenta Hydranga to do them. He had done flowers for us since Bessie's wedding. Since Bessie, Buchanan and I were paying, we insisted on Harry. The Widow promptly went to Oopsy-Daisey and ordered an ostentatious wreath for the front door. Harry did an arrangement in fall colors and hidden among the flowers was a tiny-feathered quail. Daddy loved to take his bird dogs to the woods and hunt quail. If he had been an Indian, he would have been thrilled to be headed for the happy-hunting grounds.

Those days following Daddy's death were a blur. My family stayed at Bessie's. Of course her children filled Daddy's house. In fact, our children asked permission to go upstairs to the attic one last time. We never gathered there as a family again. Before the funeral, when we met at the house, I remember one of The Widow's grandchildren coming down the stairs from my old room with her child. At that point, all of our losses, especially the loss of Daddy, were almost palatable. Thankfully, the moment passed and we all headed to the church, to the church where they were married, to Daddy's funeral.

CHAPTER 28
"It's the thought that counts." Mama

We thought, "Okay, now we can move on," but we weren't there yet. The first Christmas came and went uneventfully. The Widow spent Christmas away with her children and our families got together at Buchanan's. We gave her gifts before Christmas to take with her. Buchanan was the executor of Daddy's estate, and there were no surprises in the will. He immediately signed over to The Widow the house and the cash. Again, we thought, "OK we can have some closure now". We thought, but we were wrong.

Lori's wedding followed the June after Daddy died in November. Lori is Bessie's oldest daughter. One of my most poignant memories is Lori, sitting at Grand's bedside, holding his hand and telling him how much she wanted him to be at her wedding; that he would be the only living grandparent on her side of the family. She, like Anna Bet, had a special bond with Daddy. I guess each grandchild had their own special memories of Daddy, especially the older ones. Lori's then husband-to-be appreciated antiques and Daddy promised to give them a beautiful baby crib he had salvaged from a junk pile on the street in Charleston when he was in medical school. He later restored it. Of course, by today's standards it would be considered unsafe for a baby, but it could be a lovely addition when used like a bassinette in a living room or den where someone was around to watch a sleeping baby. In fact it is in Bessie's living room now, awaiting the arrival of her first grandchild. Thankfully, we were able to get it in time.

Since Daddy was gone Bessie felt no compulsion to include The Widow in the wedding party as grandmother-of-the-bride, yet we knew she needed to be included in some way. Mama's friends gave Lori a wonderful wedding luncheon at Caledonia where friends celebrated both the bride and Mama. The Widow's presence would be awkward. Bessie followed the wishes of Lori, Bryan, Lori's husband to be, and Lou. She simply invited The Widow to the wedding as a guest. I heard she went around town, like to Cooper's Gift Shop and tried to elicit sympathy because she was not included in the wedding party. Excuse me! Whose fault was that? Cooper almost fell for it. When she asked JoNelle about the situation, JoNelle quickly set her straight. I heard she showed up and sat on the back row, dabbing her eyes with a handkerchief...the injured Widow. She didn't even bother to show up for Leslie's wedding two years later. She tried to tell folks at the bank where Leslie worked that she hadn't been invited. Fortunately, one of the ladies' daughters helped with the invitations and could affirm that The Widow had indeed been invited. Our Mama taught us to do right.

I heard, via Me Maw, that at the Lenton Luncheon, the new preacher asked The Widow how she was kin to Bessie. I heard she sort of stammered and said, "She is my step-daughter". Me Maw reported that the new preacher asked, "Well, why weren't you at Leslie's wedding?" The Widow replied with a stammered lame-sounding excuse.

Also, there was the matter of the gravestone. . . As I said before The Widow had it centered in the gravesite... a unilateral decision, I might add. Another decision she made unilaterally was the epitaph. Under Daddy's name read, "He served his country, church, family and many other families through his medical practice."

One of Daddy's regrets was that he spent a good portion of The War in medical school and in his internship. When he finally was able to serve his country, he was stuck off in the middle of Kansas. His war stories consisted of telling how he had to stave off advances from lonely wartime Mamas. He envied Hub and Tom and his other friends who saw real action. He didn't feel he served his country through his medical practice.

The epitaph made it sound like he was a missionary, or something for the church. I believe he served God in his medical practice but went on no mission trips as such. He was never even an usher as far as I can remember.

He served our family, but not often through his medical practice. If anything his medical practice kept him away from us. He was our Daddy, NOT our doctor.

He did serve many families through his medical practice. Over the years I have heard many stories of his caring, kind-hearted, medical care. For this we were very proud of him. I have heard stories of lives he saved and stories of lives made better by his work. We suffered with him when children needed help beyond what he could give. I remember when a friend of mine's brother broke his neck in a dive into the Waccamaw River and died and when my friend Harriette's baby died. He let me know that God knew what he was doing, even when we didn't understand. He was a good doctor and a caring man. But that epitaph just did not describe Daddy. Besides, I think it was poorly worded. Oh well, she didn't ask me what I thought. Now every time I visit the gravesite I want to dig it up and change it. Maybe someday I will.

Then another Christmas came around. Since the last Christmas, none of us had really had much personal interaction with The Widow. At best, we had spoken if we saw her at Church. JoNelle and I discussed what we should do about a Christmas gift for The Widow, whether or not we should even give her one. We decided that we would be remiss not to remember her in some way, but we knew Bessie would probably disagree. Without consulting Bessie, we decided that we would send her a poinsettia. We were not being nice, though. I knew that The Widow did not like poinsettias because she had told us so one year when she showed the huge gorgeous flowers from Uncle Elmore and Aunt Clara. She said, "I don't know why they always send us a poinsettia. They are ugly and I think they grow them in moldy soil. I believe they make it hard for your daddy to breathe." I remember thinking then, "How can anyone not like poinsettias at Christmas?"

But then she was very particular about her flowers. One year, I ordered day lilies from Park Seed for her for Christmas. She told me she didn't want the kind I had ordered, that she wanted a different kind. I simply cancelled the whole thing. She also claimed not to like geraniums. Daddy had always loved tending his geranium window boxes and impatiens hanging baskets. The geraniums were replaced for a while.

After Daddy's death, someone sent a shifferlera to The Widow who promptly returned it, saying she knew that the person who sent it would have spent at least $100.00. She insisted that the one sent be replaced with a larger one. Needless to say, many florists would just as soon do without her business. When I moved back to Kingston, she sent me a shifferlera, but I don't think it was a $100.00 one.

We deliberately sent her poinsettias that Christmas but insisted that it be a large beautiful one. When JoNelle called Harry, she was very specific in her directions as to what was to be on the card. It was to be sent to The Widow, not Mrs. Buchanan Bethea, because of the confusion that often accompanied deliveries so labeled. The card was to read from JoNelle and Buchanan, Katherine and Scott and Bessie and Lou.

Imagine JoNelle's surprise when Harry called later and asked what to do about the flower. When his delivery girl tried to deliver the poinsettia, The Widow refused it. She claimed she didn't know "these people". She suggested that maybe the flower belonged to JoNelle and Buchanan. JoNelle had gone to great pains to make sure that the card was right. At that time Scott and I were in the process of moving to Kingston. Scott was staying at Kitty's house. When I was visiting, I told Kitty what happened. Kitty told Sudie Bea how surprised we were that The Widow had already forgotten us.

When the word got back to The Widow, I guess she had second thoughts about having sent the flowers back. She went downtown to the Magenta Hydrangea to try to explain away her situation. Didn't work. Bessie said, "I would have told you not to send flowers, if you had asked." She was perturbed with us for not running it by her.

CHAPTER 29
"All's well that ends well." Mama

L ater, after Scott and I were back in Kingston, The Widow was to have a big 80th birthday celebration in Columbia. One of her daughters owned a Wedding Chapel catering service. She invited all of us to the soirée. At the time we did not know that she had an ulterior motive. The unanimous response of Scott, Lou and Buchanan to the invitation was a unanimous and resounding "No!" To be very specific, I think it was "Hell no!"

We decided that to remember her birthday, which we felt we had to do, we would make a donation in her name to the church. That would not be returned and there would be a public announcement in the bulletin that we had acknowledged her birthday. She could not go out and say we ignored it. We sent our regrets, a card, and the donation. The church secretary, knowing The Widow, suggested that we leave off the birthday year. The bulletin read, "In honor of the occasion of her January 24 birthday."

Somewhere around the time of the scheduled birthday party, JoNelle was at the high school working on some parent volunteer project. She heard from another parent volunteer that The Widow had put Daddy's house up for sale. JoNelle was sure the parent was mistaken. The whole reason Daddy left The Widow the house was so she would always have a place to live. Daddy's will had not even been probated, yet. Of course, by now the house was in her name. She couldn't be already selling it, could she?

JoNelle called her good friend who worked in the county appraiser's office. She looked it up. She confirmed that the house was for sale and its price listed with a local realtor. We were again stunned. Looks like by now we would have learned! Later, she told folks that we had been given first refusal, but that was just not so.

Shortly after we heard the news, The Widow called me and asked," Can you, Bessie, and Buchanan and your spouses come over to my house Friday evening about 5:00? I would like to talk to you all." This was Thursday. I told her I would check with them and see. There was another strong unanimous negative response.

By now we were finally catching on. We knew that the purpose of the "meeting" was probably to tell us about the house being for sale. She had this tendency to do things in a dramatic way. JoNelle and I decided that I should plan ahead what I was going to say. When I called The Widow back I had written notes. We had three main points we thought we should make: (1) Let her think we thought she had an offer on the house, so that she would know we had heard it. Also let her know we knew the asking price. (2) Tell her we were sorry she had to sell it. Daddy expected her to continue to live in it. (3) Ask her if she chooses not to use any of Mama and Daddy's stuff when she moves to please give us the opportunity to buy it.

When I called her back, I immediately told her that we couldn't come that Friday, but that we figured that she had an offer on the house. She was really caught off guard, surprised that we knew so much. She said that her intention had been to announce the decision to sell the house at her birthday party.

Since we were unable to go, she had indeed planned to tell us about it Friday.

Then she wanted to know how we could have possibly heard about the house being for sale. She said that nobody was supposed to know yet. She said that she was not allowing a "For Sale" sign in the yard and that only "her" realtor would be allowed to show it, in her presence. She was really upset about the supposed leak from the realtor's office. I would hate to have been her realtor when she got back to him!

The Widow eventually sold the house to the daughter of Dr. Ambrose, Daddy's old partner and back door neighbor. After The Widow and her children went through the stuff in the house, she did call and offer us a few things. For this I guess we should be grateful. I heard about one family where the children asked to buy their wedding dresses and portraits from their stepmother. I went to the house and got what she offered. I was particularly proud to have the old dresser that belonged to Daddy when he was a boy and an old worn oriental rug that Mama and Daddy had in the den.

Mama always wanted oriental rugs but this was the only one she got...and it was a hand-me-down. Daddy would have readily bought Mama a rug, but she was too Scotch to buy one. They had bought it from one of Daddy's old best friends from Marion and The Citadel. Colonel May was in the army and didn't want to take the rug on a move.

I personally would never want to buy an oriental rug. I hate to think about all those poor children being forced to knot all those pieces of wool. When we sold some timber on the farm, I used my share to buy a nice American, machine-made rug for my dining room. It was like a memorial to Mama. Bessie and I were riding along one day with Belle in the car with us, having an animated discussion about the merits of various types of rugs when Belle said, "I don't ever want to grow up!"

"Why not?"

"I don't want to grow up because then I might like to talk about rugs."

JoNelle and Buchanan are using Mama and Daddy's old bedroom lamps. Bessie may use the bedside tables but I bet not. We had finally finished the cleaning out. The Widow closed on the sale of the house the same week Daddy's estate was settled. I hope Mama rests easier. I know Bessie, Buchanan, and I do.

EPILOGUE
"Suffer the little children to come unto me"
White Bricks
By Belle, Age 15
English Class Composition 1998

I had just gotten some new construction paper. My grandmother was sick, so I decided to draw the best picture my little, chubby fingers could draw. Of course, it was only scribble, and yes, she would have to lie and say it was the most beautiful picture she had ever seen, but maybe it would make her feel better. She had a great big brass bed sitting in the middle of the living room so her friends could all come and visit her. Everyone tells me she enjoyed people and could not bear to be locked up in a back bedroom where everyone would feel they were invading her privacy if they came to visit her. So there she was, waiting for her company as if nothing was wrong. When I walked into the living room, all the adults surrounding her bed tried to push me away and keep me from seeing my grandmother. Once she saw me, she insisted they let me in. I gave her the picture. She admired it and looked at me with the most gentle, loving smile. She was happy with my small gift, and it made me proud of what I had done. That is one of the few memories I have left of my grandmother. I remember enjoying visiting her house and enjoying seeing her, but I was so young when she died that there is little for me to remember.

When I was seven years old, my grandfather remarried a widow whom my family calls The Widow. The woman seemed nice enough to me. She didn't feel like a grandmother, but at the time it didn't seem important. She always dressed in elegant old women's clothes. She wore those big earrings that seemed to make her ears stretch all the way down to her shoulders. She had white hair, but when I was seven I considered all light hair blonde. She wore enough jewelry to show that she was definitely not poor. She always had a smile that looked like it was glued on. It was different from my grandmother's warm, loving smile. It almost was like she felt forced to be friendly towards us. Of course, all of that didn't matter to me, then. My aunt and my mother didn't let any of this go unnoticed. Although they disliked her, they felt gratitude toward her for taking care of their father, or as the grandchildren know him, "Gran."

As the years went by, it became progressively harder to visit the house. Everything lost my grandmother's spirit and began to turn into "The Widow's house." She even felt the need to put a sign in the patio that says, "The Widow's Garden." All the pictures of my cousins, my siblings, and me have now been replaced with pictures of her family. She redecorated the house to suit her. Going there was no longer like going to a familiar home. It was like staying in a hotel. Of course, I got the room with the gigantic picture of The Widow hanging in it. It was the last thing I saw when I closed my eyes to go to sleep, and it was the first thing I saw when I opened them in the morning. We rarely stayed at her house when at least one member of her family wasn't staying there too. We finally resorted to avoiding staying there when at all possible.

Whenever we go to Kingston, which is where Gran and The Widow live, we always have to go visit them for an hour or so. For a while, whenever we went there, I felt a ripping sensation in my side and stomach. I remembered when my cousins and I played in the yard and ate big dinners there. Just thinking about how that part of my life was gone made me hurt to the point that I thought I would throw up. Watching Gran, sitting in his chair, so old that he didn't have a clue how much had changed—or how old I was for that matter, just made me feel worse. She has everything: the garden that we played hide and seek in, the attic that we all carved our names in, the two fish mounted on the wall—the one whose mouth had been filled with pennies and the great blue sword fish Gran caught in the Gulf of Mexico. And what does it mean to her emotionally? It means nothing—exactly what is left for us to have when we are grown and want to reminisce about our childhood.

When I last visited Kingston, I finally realized there was no use getting angry and trying to fight to get it back. One thing made me realize this. In the den, there is an old brick fireplace, made of brick that someone in my family had salvaged from an old warehouse in Charleston. My grandmother was from Charleston. The Widow had painted the whole brick fireplace white. It is no longer as beautiful as I had always thought it was. Although it is white, I will always know red bricks are underneath all that paint. It is like my family and my grandmother. Even though you may not see us, or traces of us in the house, we will always be there somewhere. Our spirits are there, and our memories, too. You just have to know how to find them. Once you do, the white paint won't look so bad after all.